# *See You Soon Broadway*

## Broadway Series Book One

### By: Melissa Baldwin

This is a work of fiction. Names, characters, places, and
incidents either are the product of the author's
imagination or are used fictitiously, and any resemblance
to actual persons, living or dead, business establishments,
events, or locales is entirely coincidental.

ISBN: 0692508147
ISBN 13: 978-0692508145

# Other Books by Melissa Baldwin

Acknowledgements:

To my grandmothers, Mildred and Georgia, and my mother, Wendy: You are true examples of strong, faithful, and powerful women. I dedicate this book to you.

# Chapter 1

I made it. I'm finally here with the lights, the sounds, and the rush . . . I start spinning around like Julie Andrews in *The Sound of Music*. You would think one of the thousands of people on the street would stop and ask me if I was okay . . . or maybe not—after all, this is New York City. In reality, these people couldn't care less if I was okay. But really, I must look ridiculous spinning around in the middle of Times Square.

"Maris! Maris!" Awesome, someone knows my name. Maybe I'm famous now. I look around to see who's calling my name, but I'm alone. Holy crap! I'm alone in Times Square. Where did everyone go?

"Maris!" Now someone is shaking me, maybe the earth has been taken over by zombies or some nonsense like that. There's a reason I never watch those kinds of shows; I would have nightmares for days. As it is, when a commercial comes on for a scary movie, I have to close my eyes, cover my ears, and repeat "la, la, la" over and over.

"Don't kill me!" I shout and jump up.

I look around and there I am in the living room of the apartment I share with my best friend, Georgie. I must have fallen asleep on the couch.

"That must have been one hell of a dream." She smirks. "Don't you have to go to work?"

"Yes." I groan. I feel horrible; this is why I don't take naps. I always wake up groggy and in a bad mood.

"I have a few lessons this afternoon, and then I have to go to that family dinner with Kyle." I sit up slowly because if I get up too fast, I'll get dizzy. I don't know why that happens, but it does every time I get up too quickly.

"What are you doing home? I thought you were on shift?" Georgie is a nurse at the hospital and she works crazy hours, so it's a surprise seeing her home in the middle of the afternoon.

"I was," she replies dramatically as she falls back onto our Brady Bunch couch. Our couch is a tacky plaid print that looks like it is out of the 1970s, so that's why we nicknamed it the Brady Bunch couch.

"It was really slow and someone needed extra hours, so I left." She starts picking at her gel manicure like she always does when she's lying around.

I start to gather all of my materials for my lessons this afternoon. One of these days, I will get organized. I have a plan to get organized; however, I'm not organized enough to put my plan into action or something like that.

I have been teaching vocal lessons at Do-Re-Mi Studios for two years. I enjoy my job but my dream has always been to perform on Broadway. Hell, I would settle for off Broadway. Don't get me wrong, my job is very fulfilling. I have some fantastic students, and I love sharing my passion with others. But to sing on Broadway . . .

My first student this afternoon is the very adorable and precocious Sadie, a vocal and piano student. Every word she speaks comes out in song. She reminds me of myself at her age.

"Helloooo, Miss Maris," she sings when she arrives. She even does a little twirl in the lobby.

"Helloooo, Sadie," I reply. And so this begins our lesson.

Following Sadie's lesson, I have Mimi's lesson. Mimi is sixteen and a typical teenager, and she's not as fun to teach as Sadie because she thinks she knows everything already. The truth is she's fantastically talented; I'm just afraid her ego will get in the way. I once made a comment about her attitude and her mother called me and told me off. I thought for sure she wouldn't be coming back to me, but according to Lucy, the owner, I'm the best.

I never thought I would still be teaching lessons at twenty-six. My plan was always to perform, but unfortunately, sometimes life gets in the way. I really shouldn't complain; if I had run off to New York years ago, I never would have met Kyle.

Ahhh . . . yes, Kyle. I guess it's a good sign that I still get giddy over him after two years. Kyle is that guy—the guy you want to take home to your parents and definitely the guy you want to bring to your high school reunions. He's successful and attractive, but not so attractive that people would doubt his sincerity.

Anyway, I really couldn't ask for a better boyfriend. The only problem is that he's established in our lovely suburban city and has no desire to go to New York. Ever. We've had a few brief discussions about this, but I think he's been pretty clear that he doesn't see NYC in his future. I've never pushed the issue because I'm happy . . . really, I am.

After I finish up with my lessons, I head to my parents' house for our monthly family dinner. My mom insists that we all come for dinner once a month to keep our family relationships strong, which is totally silly because we all get along fine. My parents have lived in the same house since they got married, and my older sister, Cassie, and her husband, Mark, live nearby.

"Hey!" I yell when I walk in the door. I take off my boots and do what I always do when I go home: I stand at the front door, get a running start, and try to slide in my socks through the main hall on the wood floor. After I slide a few feet, I wander into the kitchen.

"What are you guys up to?" I ask. My mom and Cassie are busily looking through some boxes.

"Hi, hon. Dad was cleaning out the garage and found these boxes," Mom replies. She continues to empty some junk from a box onto the table.

"Mom and Dad are finally cleaning out their stuff. I told them that they need to feng shui," Cassie says softly.

Cassie just opened her own yoga studio; she's probably the most calm and mentally sound person I have ever met in my life. I have thought about talking to her about the possibility of me moving to New York, but I'm a little nervous about what she's going to say.

"Maris, do you remember this? We used to play restaurant with this old menu." Cassie holds up a menu that we stole from IHOP in the 80s. We used to play restaurant in Mom's Tupperware closet for hours.

"I can't believe we still have that thing," I exclaim. Although, I'm not surprised since Mom and Dad never throw anything away.

"I'm keeping this for my kids," Cassie adds. Ugh, typical Cassie—she may be calm and patient but she will always be the bossy *older* sister. She thinks she knows everything just because she's a whopping three years older than me.

"Um, why do you get to keep it and you don't even have kids yet?" I demand. She doesn't say anything; no doubt she is chanting some kind of yoga stuff in her mind to ease the tension that's building.

"You're right," she replies calmly. "We should share this once we both have kids, of course."

I guess I can't really argue with her considering she's definitely closer to having kids than I am.

I start looking through a box that's on the floor. It looks like a bunch of old stuff that belonged to my grandmother. Grandma passed away two years ago and my parents got the remainder of her things. I sort through the box of romance novels, crossword puzzles, and *National Geographics* from thirty years ago. As I'm sorting through the stuff, I find a red leather-bound notebook at the bottom of the box. My curiosity is building as I run my fingers over the gorgeous worn leather. I open it to the first page and immediately recognize my grandmother's handwriting.

The first page is dated March 10, 1948 . . .

"What's that?" Cassie asks, staring at the notebook.

"I'm not sure. It looks like a journal. I think it was Grandma's." I hold it up and show them, carefully keeping a tight grip on it. I don't want Cassie to play the oldest child card and claim it for herself.

"I've never seen that before," my mom says curiously. "Of course, that isn't much of a surprise; Mother was a bit of a mystery sometimes."

Now I'm totally intrigued. My grandmother was an interesting woman, very educated and well spoken. I was named after her, so I always felt a connection to her because of that. I remember her well because she used to visit us a lot when we were younger, when she wasn't on one of her trips with her girlfriends. My grandpa passed away when I was really young, so I don't remember much about him.

The doorbell interrupts my thoughts. My excitement starts to build, as I know that must be Kyle.

"I'll get it!" both Cassie and I yell and make a run for the door.

We both slide on the wood floor as we race for the door. Sure enough, it's Kyle waiting politely at the door with a bottle of wine in hand. He always brings something to dinner; he says his mother always taught him never to show up at a dinner party empty-handed.

"Hello, Kyle, it's wonderful to see you," Cassie says warmly.

"Same to you, Cassie," he says politely. He gives me a big smile and I melt. I never really understood that term "melt." What does that even mean?

I give him a big hug and grab his hand as we head back to the kitchen. Kyle could possibly be the best boyfriend ever, well, except for that one teeny-tiny difference of opinion when it comes to moving.

After dinner (and too much wine), my parents start talking. I can tell by the way they had their heads together throughout the night that they were gearing up for something big.

"We have some exciting news for you girls," Dad says as he reaches for Mom's hand.

I knew it! My mind starts to wander; this could be really exciting, unless of course they tell us they are expecting a baby. I start to imagine Mom being pregnant at the same time as Cassie. They would have to have a joint baby shower and I would have to throw it. My throat starts to tighten and my palms start sweating. I'm not even sure why this random thought popped into my head.

"Since I'm officially retiring in June, your mother and I have decided to sell the house," he exclaims excitedly.

What did he say? Sell our house? This is insane. This is the house I grew up in, the house where I spent my childhood.

"No!" I yell louder than I intended. "You can't!"

"Maris, calm down," Mom says calmly. "This really is exciting news. We're looking at condos over on the coast. Remember when we used to spend summers there? Those were some wonderful trips."

"The coast? But that's miles away!"

Cassie hasn't said a word, which could mean two things: either she's in shock or she already knew about this.

"Cassie, what do you think? Please tell me that you aren't okay with this?" I can already tell by her body language that she's already at peace with this news. I don't doubt that she's already had time to meditate or yoga her way through it.

"I agree this news isn't the best, but I feel that it's a great idea for Mom and Dad to retire to the ocean," she says thoughtfully. "Congratulations, you two!" She and Mark get up to give our parents hugs. Kyle looks at me and gives me a concerned smile.

"You okay?" he whispers. I don't really know what I am. I mean, I haven't lived in this house in years but it was always nice to know that it was here if I ever needed to come home.

"I think so," I reply as he puts his arm around me. "Just a little surprised; although, there could be worse news." I don't tell him anything about my imagining Mom and Cassie's joint baby shower. I decide I need to apologize for my childish outburst.

"Mom, Dad, I'm sorry," I say. "You guys have worked toward this for years so . . . um, congratulations."

Ugh! That didn't sound convincing at all. I must be the worst daughter ever. My parents don't seem to notice my awkward reaction. Somehow about a gazillion photos of beachfront condos have magically appeared. Everyone seems to be very interested in looking at them except for me. I mindlessly glance at each photo and pass them to Kyle who is sitting to my left. How is this happening so fast? I look around at the slightly worn wallpaper and the slippery wood floors. I can't believe I will have to say good-bye to my childhood home. Do I have some sort of weird attachment issues that have never been diagnosed?

I'm a little surprised at the number of photos they have; it seems like this has been in the works for a while.

"So, when did you guys decide to do this?" I ask innocently. Cassie looks up from the photo she's holding. I can tell by her expression that she's silently trying to cleanse my aura, or maybe she's just mentally judging me. Thankfully, my parents are oblivious to our silent communication.

"Believe it or not, we have talked about this for years," my dad replies. "After you girls moved out, we realized that we'd love to downsize and enjoy our retirement. No more lawn to mow or weeds to pull."

Who is this man and what has he done with my father? My father loved spending hours on the lawn every weekend.

"Oh, and don't you girls forget that you both have boxes of your things in the attic."

Ah yes, how could I forget about all my boxes? I can't believe my childhood memories will soon be reduced to a few boxes of things. All of this change is giving me anxiety, and there's only one thing for me to do when this happens . . . sing. I've been doing this for a while. There's a little park just around the corner from my apartment. When I want to just let go and relax, I go and sing. I sing everything from Broadway show tunes to gangster rap. Yes, really!

At the end of the night, I'm pretty quiet as Kyle and I walk out together.

"You want to talk? I can come over or you can come to my place?" he asks sympathetically.

I would love to stay up all night talking to him, but I don't know what to think or say. With my parents moving farther away, this is all the more reason for me to consider moving also. I don't quite know how to bring up the New York issue again, but I know I need to. However, tonight I really just want to get to that park.

"I would love to but I'm kind of tired. How about lunch tomorrow?" I wrap my arms around his waist.

"You sure?" he asks. I can tell he knows what I'm up to. "You want to go to the park, don't you?"

Busted.

Kyle has joined me in the park a few times. For the longest time I never told anyone, but one night after Kyle dropped me off, I left my phone in his car and when he came back to bring it to me, he saw me sneak around the corner. I had no choice but to reveal my deep dark secret. Not that it's dark or even a secret really. Plenty of strangers have stopped to listen to me. Thankfully, I'm not afraid to sing in front of people. One night, a couple asked why I didn't have a jar out for tips. Maybe I should? I could probably make some pretty decent cash.

"I was thinking about it," I say nonchalantly. He totally knows that I have every intention of going to the park.

"I can come and sit with you if you want." See, best boyfriend ever. I must be crazy to consider moving away from him. I know that long-distance relationships usually don't work. Why would I even risk losing him?

"Thanks. You're the best, but I think I need to be alone tonight." I do my best not to make him feel bad, and thankfully he understands.

When I get home, I park my car in front of my apartment and leisurely walk around the corner. I sit down on the bench and close my eyes. When I open my eyes, I start to belt out "For Good" from *Wicked*. I then go through a medley of songs from *Les Mis*, *Annie*, and *Hairspray*.

I immediately start to feel better. Cassie can have all her downward dogs and chair poses; thankfully, I have my singing. I reach into my bag to grab my phone when my hand touches something. It's the journal I found earlier. I totally forgot about it after my parents' big announcement. My curiosity takes control, and I hurry home so I can read it.

# Chapter 2

"I can't believe they're selling their house. I always thought they would be there forever," Georgie says after I tell her about my parents. I think she's even more shocked than I was. I probably should have just waited until the next day to tell her.

"But, it's the end of an era!" she exclaims. She wants to sit there and talk about every detail of their move, and I just want to go lie down and read my grandmother's journal. It's as if it's burning a hole in my bag. I haven't been this excited to read since the fourth *Twilight* book was released.

"I know; I'm pretty exhausted." I'm hoping she will get the hint. I could always tell her about the journal, but then she will want to read it too.

"You went to the park, didn't you? I don't blame you." She didn't get my hint. "What did Guru Cassie have to say?"

I let out a frustrated sigh. She isn't going to let it go, so

I may as well sit and talk to her.

What seems like hours go by when Georgie finally stops with the million questions. I head to my room when my phone rings. I see that it's Cassie calling. I let it go to voicemail because I already know what she's going to say. I'm about to open the journal when she calls again. Seriously, this girl has to get up in four hours for her meditation. Why does she keep calling?

"Hello?" I finally answer.

"I knew you were still awake," she says immediately.

I scowl. "Well, I wouldn't be if someone wasn't calling me over and over again. Shouldn't you be asleep by now?"

"Yes, I should be, but I felt like we should talk." Here comes my lecture. "I know the news was shocking for you. I was also shocked when I first found out. A few weeks ago, I stopped by to bring Mom some kale chips I made and I answered a phone call from a realtor. My first reaction was similar to yours, but I've had the time to get used to it." She continues talking but, admittedly, I'm still focused on the kale chips—gross.

"I felt like you needed to know so you didn't feel like you were the only one to be unhappy about it."

"Thanks," I say softly. "So, are you and Mark going to stay nearby?" The temptation to bring up my New York idea is overpowering.

"Oh, yes! I'm having way too much fun with the house, and we're established here, no reason to leave." Cassie and Mark bought an old farmhouse and they've been renovating it. I'm actually impressed with all they've done; I was very skeptical when they first bought it because, honestly, it was a dump.

"Oh good."

"How about you?" she asks. "Things seem to be moving along nicely with Kyle." And there it is, my perfect window to ask my all-knowing sister what I should do with my life.

"Yes! Kyle is great." I hesitate, not because I don't think he's great, but because he is. I just don't know what to say or how to bring it up. Lucky for me, my sister is very in tune with everything around her.

"But?" she asks. "Go ahead and tell me what you're thinking."

"Well—you remember when I had that wild idea to move to New York and pursue my performing career? Life happened and I met Kyle. He has no desire to ever move and I don't know . . . I guess it's been on my mind again." I finally stop to take a breath and wait for her response.

"Wow. Really?" She seems really surprised. "I thought you had moved on from that? I mean, you haven't mentioned it in a while." She stops talking and, unlike her, I don't have the power to read other people's minds or their energies.

"Do you think I'm crazy?" I ask finally.

"Crazy? Of course I don't think that. But I do think

you have to search for your answer," she says thoughtfully.

Search? What does she mean by search? Like on Google?

"Um, okay?"

"You need to search within yourself. Ask yourself for the answer to this life-changing question. What do you really want?"

I'm more confused than ever. "Are you asking me this or telling me to ask myself?"

I can hear the frustration as she lets out a big sigh. "I have faith in you that you will make the right decision."

I know that means she's tired of talking to me. I glance at the clock next to my bed. Ugh! I can feel my eyes start to close, so I do us both a favor and get off the phone.

I close my eyes for two seconds then I remember Grandma's journal. I really want to read, but I'm so tired—maybe just a page or two.

*March 10, 1948*

*I have been meaning to begin this journal for weeks. A birthday gift from my lovely friend Beatrice, according to her I must make a record of my endeavors. I suppose I should make her proud. So I will do so.*

*What a day I had today. Perhaps my hours, days, and years of rehearsals will pay off after all. I auditioned at one of New York City's top radio stations today. Truthfully, it's difficult to fathom that I, Maris Goodwin, could actually perform on the radio.*

*They told me that I sounded lovely and that they would be in contact. Tonight, I'm planning on staring out my window to watch for shooting stars; that would be my greatest wish—to be able to perform on the radio.*

Wow. Just wow. How did I not know any of this about my grandmother? I knew that she sang in church, but I had no idea that she auditioned for a radio station. I read on until I can barely hold my eyes open.

~*~*~

I hear my phone ringing from somewhere under my covers. Crap! I totally forgot to charge it after my phone call with Cassie. I glance at the clock, 7:15.

"Hello?" I wonder if I sound as bad as I think.

"Morning, my dear, Lucy here. Terribly sorry for the early wake-up call."

*No, she's not,* I think to myself. I don't actually say that out loud because I have no desire to get on Lucy's bad side. I sit up so I don't sound like I'm completely hung over.

"Hi, Lucy." I clear my throat as quietly as I possibly can. "It's totally fine. What can I do for you?"

I wish she wouldn't have called so early because I'm still half asleep and I only hear half of what she's saying regarding our end-of-year recital. That is until she says something that grabs my attention.

"Now for the exciting news!" she exclaims. I think this woman has already had five cups of coffee. "I have made arrangements to have a few agents fly in from New York for the show. This could be a huge opportunity for a few of our superstars and for the studio. Don't you think?"

Agents? Oh my gosh!

"Yes!" I shout. "I mean, this is so exciting, for everyone." Suddenly, I'm wide-awake.

She continues talking about the recital, but I have completely zoned out. Not only is this a chance to show off my students and all of their hard work, but also Lucy gives each instructor a chance to showcase our own talents at the recital. After we hang up, I practically leap out of my bed. I have a lot of work to do.

~*~*~

Several hours later, I'm still hard at work on my grand plan. I have another little secret that I haven't told anyone. I actually started writing my own songs a few years ago. Every once in a while I will work on them, but now with a goal in mind, I think I can finally finish one. I would love to perform one of my original songs in the showcase. While I'm sitting at my keyboard, something catches the corner of my eye. I look over to see my grandmother's journal still sitting on my nightstand.

"Maris? Are you home?" I hear Georgie call out.

"In here."

Georgie walks in wearing her hot pink scrubs. She says those are the best pair to wear when the *dashing* resident doctors are on shift.

"Guess who asked me out today?" she raises her eyebrows.

"Hmm . . . my guess would be one of the many hot residents? You know I can't remember names."

"Are you kidding me? You can't remember Dr. Scott? I have only talked about him every minute of every day for two months." She rolls her eyes, but in my defense, she knows I don't keep track of the drama of her hospital or the continuing saga of her love life.

"Dr. Scott or Dr. McHotty?" I let out a little giggle.

"You have no idea! Well, Scott is his first name but everyone calls him Dr. Scott. Ahhh . . ." She lets out a big sigh and falls back on my bed as if she's madly in love. "Anyway, Dr. Scott has invited me to this fabulous ritzy rooftop charity benefit this weekend, and he told me to invite some friends. So, do you and Kyle want to join us?"

I can see the exhilaration in her eyes. She loves that kind of stuff.

"I think so, but I will check with Kyle just to make sure."

Georgie was in a relationship for three years with her college boyfriend. I was sure they were going to get married but they broke up rather suddenly. Georgie says they just grew apart, but I still wonder if there's more to the story. Anyway, she's been serial dating for a while now. She claims that with her crazy schedule she can't commit to a relationship, but I'm not buying that.

"Whatcha working on over here?" She finally notices that I'm hard at work at my keyboard. I subtly move my music sheets under some songbooks. I don't feel like getting into all of that. It's not that I have stage fright exactly, but it can be nerve-wracking when it's your own material.

"End-of-year recital pieces," I say quickly. "It's going to be a huge event this year. Lucy is bringing in some big-time agents from New York." I'm practically bouncing out of my chair because I'm dying to tell Georgie that I'm planning to use this event as an audition for myself. I know that if I say anything I will open a huge can of worms and I will have to face the dilemma that's staring me in the face.

"Really?" she says thoughtfully. "That's exciting, maybe you should talk to one of them about getting you some gigs?"

What did she say? Is she a mind reader, too? Has she been hanging out with Cassie behind my back?

"Why do you say that?" I ask nonchalantly.

"Seriously, Maris? You're one of the most talented people I know, and you have wanted to perform since

I don't know—birth? So, why not?"

I don't know how to respond to this? I mean, I guess I could tell her what I've been thinking but I wonder if I should talk to Kyle first.

"Well, maybe." I hesitate. "I mean, it's kind of hard to get gigs when I'm not living in the city?"

I look at her as I secretly hope she will give me an answer, any answer, on what to do. I catch myself holding my breath, so I let it out.

"Yeah, you're probably right," she says. Unfortunately, she didn't follow my lead. "So, when are we going shopping for this party? I need a new outfit, something hot, something that screams *doctor's girlfriend.*"

I try not to show my disappointment, and we make plans to take a shopping trip. I text Kyle to make sure he's free the night of the party, and he says yes, of course, being the perfect boyfriend that he is.

I start to daydream about Kyle. I hate to admit that I met him at a bar, even though it's actually a very upscale bar/restaurant. Because of this I usually tell people that it was a restaurant. Anyway, we were there celebrating a friend's pinning ceremony. There were five of us girls and Kyle was at the next table with four of his friends. How perfect could those numbers be, right? Anyway, one of his friends made a joke about fate bringing the ten of us together on that night in time. Kyle didn't say much and neither did I, but he was definitely the guy that caught my eye. He told me later that he thought the same thing about me. The five of them ended up joining our table and we had an absolute blast. Two of us girls are still dating two of them and one couple got married, so I guess fate could have had something to do with it.

When I awake from my daydream, I get back to my song writing. I already have songs picked out for all my students, and truthfully, I know Mimi is ready. I would love to bring them all together to do a medley. Thankfully, Lucy gives each instructor creative control over our own students. I think that's why our shows are so dynamic.

Before my lessons for the day, I want to run to the park to practice one of my songs. As I'm gathering my things, I glance at Grandma's journal still sitting on my nightstand. For some reason, I have the feeling that I was meant to find it, and I can't wait to learn more about this fascinating person. I quickly hide it under my mattress—just in case—and run out the door.

# Chapter 3

Wow, we do look hot! We stand in front of the full-length mirror that's hanging in our hallway. Georgie and I had a very successful shopping trip and we're getting ready for the rooftop benefit. Apparently, this charity bash is just as VIP as Georgie thought it was going to be because even Lucy is attending.

"So, Dr. Scott says he will introduce us to everyone tonight," she says excitedly. "You never know who we might get to meet."

She slips on her very expensive little black dress. I think it cost her at least two paychecks.

"Let me ask you something. Are you ever going to call him just Scott?" I ask curiously. She gives me an odd look as if I've asked her something completely ridiculous.

"Everyone calls him Dr. Scott," she says firmly.

I want to respond with the ever appropriate "if

everyone jumped off a bridge" question. Instead, I just keep my big mouth shut.

We finish all of our primping just in time for Kyle to arrive. Georgie is giving him the rundown of the party when Dr. Scott arrives.

Wow. She wasn't kidding; Dr. Scott is very handsome and extremely friendly. Kyle and he instantly connect, and I can see the excitement in Georgie's eyes. She would love for us to all become best friends. I can see the wheels turning; I'm sure she has visions of us being neighbors, having BBQs, our kids playing soccer, and taking vacations together.

I haven't said a single word to Georgie regarding my thoughts of a possible move. It's not like I'm avoiding it exactly. It's . . . well, okay, I guess I am avoiding it.

Georgie takes Dr. Scott on a tour of our apartment, leaving Kyle and me to have a few minutes alone.

"You look great as usual," Kyle says, checking out my outfit. My thoughts are interrupted by his warm smile. He really has the best smile, so calming and sincere. I must have serious issues; I would be crazy to give up this life. Kyle is everything I need.

"Thanks! I'm actually looking forward to this party. According to Georgie, it's going to be pretty mem-orable." I wrap my arms around his neck and give him a passionate kiss.

"Nice! What was that for?" he asks curiously. "Not that I mind, trust me."

"Just because you're wonderful."

"Enough of that mushy stuff; let's go," Georgie says, interrupting our private moment. She winks at me as she pulls Dr. Scott out the door.

~*~*~

There are no words to describe this event. I've seen parties like this in movies but I've never actually been anywhere like this. After we arrive, we're escorted to the roof. Our tour guide checks us in and we're given swag bags. (Swag bags!) Georgie gives me a smug "I told you so" look. I just nod my head because I'm still a bit speechless.

The roof is decorated with twinkling lights with sheer white fabric cascading down from somewhere. There are soft white velvet couches everywhere. There's a live band playing in front of a small dance floor. Kyle and Dr. Scott have become best friends and have discussed everything from football to cooking.

Georgie and I already checked out the goodies in our swag bags, very subtly of course. After an hour, a few drinks, and many introductions by Dr. Scott, I excuse myself to go the restroom. On my way back, I wander around the roof and stare out at the sunset; it really is a beautiful spring night. I love this time of year in Northern Virginia, and I know I would miss it if I moved. I think I know what I need to do; I need to stay here with Kyle, Georgie, and my sister. This is my home even if my parents sell their house.

I must still be daydreaming as I quickly turn around and run smack into a man, spilling his drink all over his obviously very expensive suit.

"Oh crap! I'm so sorry," I yell. I start brushing my hand along his suit coat. Crap, what am I doing touching this man? I finally glance up at his face and wow—tall, dark hair, and very . . . um . . . masculine. I must be staring because I don't even realize that I'm still brushing the front of his coat and now his pants. I'm beyond humiliated now.

"Please don't worry. It's fine." He smiles, holding up his hands. "I mean, it's only a brand-new suit, but hey, that's what dry cleaners are for, right?"

"Um, right." I hesitate. "Sorry for um, brushing, um." *Really, Maris, shut up,* I think to myself.

He holds out his hand. "Trevor Ericson."

"Hi, I'm Maris Forrester." I shake his hand and smile thankfully. I really appreciate him changing the subject from my invading his personal space.

"Maris? That a nickname?" he asks curiously.

"No, a family name actually; I'm named after my grandmother." He has managed to find a few cocktail napkins lying around and wipes off his coat.

"That's a cool name. So, how do you know the Phillips?"

Phillips? What's he talking about?

"The Phillips?" I ask, trying not to cringe that I was rubbing the front of his suit for what seemed like five minutes.

"Yes, Tom and Liv, our hosts for this event?" He seems shocked that I have no idea who Tom and Liv are. I guess I should know that but too late now. Suddenly, I feel guilty like I just crashed a wedding or something.

"Oh right, I don't actually—we were invited by a mutual friend. It's a great party though," I say as I glance around.

"Yes, they do this every year to benefit the arts. It's such a shame so many schools are removing them from their schedules. Liv, of course, has such a passion for this cause being that she's also a musician. She's performed all over the world."

"She was a performer?" I ask excitedly. "That's fantastic. I'm a singer, too, or at least I was, now I'm a vocal instructor."

"Really? That's interesting, why don't you sing anymore?"

Should I be having this conversation with a perfect stranger? He just keeps asking me questions. I probably shouldn't be rude considering I just spilled alcohol all over his Armani suit. Okay, so I don't know for sure that it's Armani, maybe Versace? I'm not exactly up-to-date on what designers men are wearing being that Kyle is more of a Gap kind of guy.

"You know how it is, life I guess. Anyway, where did Liv perform?"

"With some orchestra, she's an amazing violin player. I went to college with Tom; we are fraternity brothers."

I roll my eyes, figures that Trevor was a frat boy. He's totally charming and outgoing, he was probably the president, too.

"Did you just give me an eye roll?" he asks playfully. I guess that was pretty obvious.

I laugh. "Yes. I was just thinking that I could totally see you being a frat boy."

He cracks a smile. "I take offense to that, but I guess the choir girls don't really like frat boys, do they? I may have to send you my dry cleaning bill after all." I start to feel uncomfortable. My amazing boyfriend is somewhere around here waiting for me and I'm chatting (not flirting) with some random frat boy.

"I'm just kidding," he says, patting my arm. "So, would you like to meet Liv? I can introduce you; it sounds like you have a lot in common. She's around here somewhere with my girlfriend."

His what? Did he say girlfriend? Ohhh . . . of course he has a girlfriend! I'm such an idiot.

"Um sure. I just have to find my friends and my *boyfriend*. They're probably looking for me considering I went to the restroom an hour ago." I emphasize boyfriend, and of course he doesn't bat an eye.

"No problem, bring them all. Liv and Tom are great."

As I start looking around for my friends, I'm feeling

extremely guilty. I must be a horrible person; I was really enjoying talking to Trevor and he seemed genuinely interested in talking to me, too. Maybe it was my imagination but he was asking me questions about my name and my singing. He was totally flirting, or at least it seemed that way.

"There you are. We were wondering what happened." Kyle comes over and grabs my hand.

"Sorry! I was just kind of wandering around and then I ran into someone and spilt his champagne all over his suit." I shake my head. "That's what I get for daydreaming."

"Oh no! Who was it?" Georgie asks worriedly. She's sitting very close to Dr. Scott who has his arm tightly wrapped around her shoulders. They really do make a cute couple.

"Don't know, his name is Trevor Ericson," I say nonchalantly. "Anyway, he's friends with Tom and Liv Phillips, they're the hosts, and he offered to introduce us to them. Apparently, Liv is behind this whole event. She's a concert violinist and has performed all over the world. I can't wait to meet her."

There, I think I did a great job taking the subject off the guy I ran into (Trevor).

"I've played golf with Tom Phillips a few times. He's a great guy," Dr. Scott chimes in. "Let's go find them."

We're on our way to meet our gracious hosts when Georgie links her arm in mine. "What's going on?" she whispers.

"Nothing," I say innocently. "I told you."

She gives me a look that clearly says she doesn't believe me.

Just then, I see Trevor talking to two very attractive women. One is very short and one is very tall.

"The one and only Dr. Scott. How are you, man?" A loud boisterous man yells, interrupting my deadpan stare at Trevor and the two women.

Georgie was right; I guess everyone does call him Dr. Scott.

"Tom! Great party." Dr. Scott introduces us to him and Tom calls Liv over. Trevor and the tall woman follow.

"My wife Liv," Tom says, giving a little bow in front of her.

We all introduce ourselves and then Trevor interrupts.

"Liv, this is the singer I was telling you about."

"Pleasure to meet you," Liv says kindly. "It actually is a small world; I'm a friend of Lucy's. Trevor was just telling us about you when Lucy mentioned you teach at her studio. You must be very good because Lucy only works with the best."

"Oh, thank you." I smile gratefully. "And thank you for organizing this event, it's such an important cause."

I glance at Trevor who is introducing himself to my

friends.

"And this is my girlfriend, Giselle," he says proudly.

Hmmm . . . Giselle. Trevor and Giselle are obviously the perfect couple. They're both attractive and confident. No doubt that they turn heads wherever they go.

Giselle gives a half smile but doesn't say much other than hello. I get an uncomfortable feeling when she turns to me. I can usually tell when people don't like me and this girl doesn't like me.

"You must be the one with champagne spill," she says smugly as she shakes my hand.

Bitch.

"I know, I'm so clumsy but I suppose that's what I get for daydreaming and not looking where I was going." I laugh nervously and glance at Trevor.

"No harm done," Trevor says calmly. Giselle gives him a dirty look and doesn't say another word to any of us. She suddenly becomes very interested in something on her phone.

I overhear Kyle and Dr. Scott planning a golf game with Tom, and Georgie seems very intrigued by my brief conversation with Giselle. She must sense the same awkwardness that I'm feeling.

"So, Maris, do you do any performing anymore?" Liv asks, saving me from Giselle and her evil glances.

"Not really, I spend most of my time working with my students. I will, however, be singing at our end-of-year recital. Lucy always gives us instructors an opportunity to do that."

"Oh yes, I have some friends from New York attending that. I hear there is some outstanding talent to be seen. I would be happy to put you in touch with them if you would like. It never hurts to get your name out there."

I think I may have just died. I should have known that Liv knows these people, and she's offered to put us in contact. Perhaps I should make her my new best friend.

Liv and Tom excuse themselves as they're pulled away by more of their guests. Dr. Scott takes Georgie to meet some of his colleagues, leaving Kyle and me with Trevor and Giselle. This is definitely one of the most awkward moments for me. Since this awkward meeting is my fault, I speak up to break the tension.

"Well, it was great meeting you, and I apologize again for the champagne." I hold out my hand to shake.

"It was nice meeting you also, best of luck in your career." He takes my hand, giving me a friendly smile, and then turns to Kyle and shakes his hand.

"Nice to meet you, Giselle," I say kindly.

"Oh, same here," she says, barely looking up from her phone as she pulls Trevor away. That was obviously not sincere but Kyle doesn't seem to notice. Typical, men are so clueless sometimes.

"Finally, I get some alone time with my girl," Kyle says after they've left. "You okay?" He pushes my hair behind my ear. "You seem preoccupied."

"Yes, I'm great," I say, wrapping my arms around his neck. There's just a lot going on with my parents' move and the recital."

"I know." He gives me a comforting smile. "I'm sure it will all work out though." He lifts my chin and kisses me and then pulls me in for a hug. In the distance, I see Trevor and Giselle in what looks like an argument. That's interesting—I wonder what that's all about?

After we arrive home, I hurry to take off my makeup and crawl into bed. As much fun as the party was, I'm more confused than ever. I had basically decided I was not going to pursue New York, and then I met Trevor and now I'm having second thoughts again. Not because of Trevor, of course, but because meeting Trevor led too meeting Liv. I never would have met her if I hadn't run into him, so I guess it was meant to be. As I'm falling asleep, I remember my grandmother's journal; I haven't looked at in in days. *Hopefully tomorrow,* I think to myself as I fall asleep.

# Chapter 4

"Thank you all for meeting this morning," Lucy says excitedly. "First up on the agenda, I want to get the schedule mapped out for the show." She takes a long sip of her coffee; I'm guessing her fourth or fifth cup already today.

Lucy called an emergency meeting to work on the schedule for the recital and start planning the after party. I can tell she means business with today's meeting, and I'm fully expecting to be here for a while. She has a full spread of food as well as a cooler full of drinks and lots of coffee. She's wearing the Juicy Couture velvet sweatsuit that she always wears when she's planning on having a long day.

"So, considering we have some very important guests who will be attending, let's do a fun and appropriate theme. I'm thinking Broadway."

OMG! I can hardly contain my excitement. If it weren't so early in the morning, I would probably get up and start dancing on her desk. All of a sudden, I've never been so excited for one of Lucy's meetings. I can tell the other instructors don't share my excitement.

There are three other main instructors at Do-Re-Mi other than me. Lilly is one of our piano teachers; she's a musical genius but probably the least social of my co-workers, or of anyone I have ever met really. She doesn't have much to do with any of us, but she's amazing with her students. I've worked with her for a few years now, but I don't remember ever having a long conversation with her.

Ash also teaches piano and vocal and she's Lucy's shadow. She basically kisses her ass and I have no doubt she's behind the breakfast spread. We've had an odd working relationship; she's always hanging around when I'm working with my students or rehearsing. We had a little bit of an issue a while back when she copied one of my ideas for a show, but I think we've moved on from it since then, or at least I've moved on. She's one of those people that you never know if you can fully trust her.

Sophie is my favorite; she can play practically every instrument and she sings. If anyone should have a performing career, it's her and she doesn't even realize how talented she is.

Several hours later, we finally agree on a tentative schedule for the recital. I'm exhausted, and by the end of the meeting, I'm ready to push Ash out the closest window. I guess she really believed this recital was going to be all about her?

When I finally get home after my long day, I fall down on my bed. I'm about to doze off when I remember my grandmother's journal. I quickly jump up and lift up my mattress. I'm not exactly sure why I hid the journal under the mattress. It's probably because when I was a teenager I used to put my diary under the mattress to keep it hidden from Cassie and my mom. I know they knew it was there but it just became a habit. As I lift the mattress, the red leather book is still lying there waiting for me to open it.

*March 20, 1948*

*Today was the official first day of spring; however, snow fell from the gray sky here in New York City. I'm hoping spring will actually make an appearance soon. It has been a dreadfully long winter.*

*I had another wonderful day today. I was asked back to the radio station for a follow-up audition. How thrilling that if I am offered the job I will be able to choose my own music. Singing is my greatest love.*

*Beatrice is most supportive and so are my dear parents. They have reminded me how important it is to follow my dreams and my heart. I'm so very tired tonight, so I must turn in.*

I read through several more pages, and I'm enthralled with learning more about this side of my grandmother. She never mentioned any of this, at least not to me. I'm hoping my mom will know more.

"Hi, Mom," I say cheerfully when she answers.

"Oh, honey, I'm glad you called. Don't forget you need to come over to look through your boxes. I'm planning a big yard sale in a few weeks, so if you have anything to sell, that would be the perfect time."

"Ugh." I groan. I keep forgetting about this stupid move. "I've been really busy, but I will come by soon."

I can tell she's preoccupied with something because she's breathing heavy and I hear a lot of rustling.

"Mom, I wanted to ask you some questions about Grandma, mainly about her radio career."

"Oh goodness. I had forgotten about that."

Seriously? How could she forget about something like this? This has to be the most exciting thing to ever happen to our family. Other than when my dad won a trip to the Grand Canyon. On the whole, our family is pretty boring.

"I had no idea about any of this," I reply.

"Well, she didn't mention it that often. I know she loved that time in her life though." She adds, "Honey, what's brought on all the questions?"

I hesitate about reminding her that I found the journal. I don't want her to ask for it back, and I definitely don't want Cassie to get her greedy hands on it. I'm pretty sure that at some point down the road we will end up having a showdown over the IHOP menu.

"Um, just curious," I say nonchalantly. "I guess I just feel a strong connection being that she was a singer and so am I, or um, was."

"Oh yes, Mother was so proud of your talents. I know

she told all of her friends about you." She adds, "Which reminds me, you know who may know more about her radio career would be her friend Beatrice."

Beatrice? No way, could she be referring to the Beatrice who gave Grandma the journal?

"Where is she? Is she still alive?" I ask excitedly. "Do you know how to get in touch with her?"

"Yes, I have her information. Mother and she rarely saw each other in their later years, but I always sent her Christmas cards and she did the same. She doesn't live too far, maybe thirty minutes away? Last I heard, she was still very healthy but that was a while ago."

That's it! I have to talk to her. I can hardly contain my excitement. My hands are shaking as I write down Beatrice's information. I'm not sure what to do. Maybe I should write her a letter instead of calling her.

My phone starts ringing and I see that it's Kyle, so I answer.

"Baby, let's go celebrate!" Kyle exclaims as soon as I answer. "I have amazing news."

"What?" I ask excitedly.

"Remember I told you that I heard one of the partners was leaving the firm?" he asks. Kyle works for an accounting firm that has been in business for many years. The original partners were friends of his grandparents.

"Yes."

"Well, the rumor was true and they have asked me to move up to that position. I'm a partner!" he yells. I think I even hear him start to cry. "I'm"—sniff—"just"—sniff—"so happy."

Holy crap, he's crying.

"That's fantastic!" I exclaim. I know how badly he wanted this. I can't help but wonder how this will affect whatever decision I make.

When I get off the phone, I stare at Beatrice's number in my hand. There's no need to drag this out. I grab my phone and dial her number.

My heart is beating so fast I can almost hear it pounding. An answering machine picks up with a generic message. I almost hang up, but I instead decide to leave a message.

"Um, hi. I'm sorry to bother you. My name is Maris Forrester and my grandmother was Maris Goodwin. I got your information from my mother and . . ."

"Hello?" someone answers.

"Um, hello?"

"This is Beatrice Anderson, what a nice surprise to receive your phone call," she says happily. "I like to screen my phone calls because those damn people are always trying to sell me something. I can't tell you how many calls I get about adding a water purifying system on my house. Come on, I'm 89 years old, do you think I care if I'm drinking shitty water?"

I laugh. I can already tell that I'm going to like her. "I guess not." I agree. She continues on about the different companies that call her and I don't want to interrupt her.

"So, what can I do for you?" she finally asks.

"Well, I actually wanted to talk to you about my grandmother. I guess you two were close friends, right?" I want to feel her out because I never heard of her before finding the journal, so I'm not sure if they stayed in regular contact.

"Yes, we were—at one time. We met in college. Maris was a dear girl, very smart and talented."

I let out a sigh of relief. This may be easier than I thought.

"Unfortunately, I can't talk long now. My grandson will be here shortly to take me to an appointment."

"Oh, that's fine," I reply. "When would be a good time for me to call you back?"

"Would you like to join me for lunch? How about Saturday?" she asks eagerly.

"That sounds great!" I say excitedly. She seems really happy that I accepted her invitation. I write down her address, and we hang up.

I can't wait for Saturday.

~*~*~

"I want to make a toast, to my amazing girlfriend!" Kyle says, holding up his wine glass. "You've always been so supportive of me. I can't even count the hours that you listened to me go on and on about my work. I want to thank you for your patience because I even annoy myself sometimes. I'm so lucky that you continue to put up with me."

I stare at his handsome face; he really is so dreamy. I hold up my wine glass and we toast. We've had a great night so far. I decide to tell him about Beatrice because I was so excited about our phone call. I also tell him all about the journal, otherwise he would probably wonder why I was so excited to go to lunch with some old lady.

"What a cool story. I can't believe you never knew she was a radio performer," he says. "So, what other information are you hoping to find out?"

"I'm not sure exactly," I say thoughtfully. "I guess I'm just really curious. I mean, it's kind of fascinating to learn that someone I knew and loved had a whole other life. It's almost like uncovering a mystery."

He nods his head. "Yeah, and you never know what else you may uncover."

He's right, although I don't know what else there could be. For all I knew, Grandma lived a normal life raising a family in the suburbs.

"How are things at the studio?" he asks.

I give him the up-to-date rundown about our recital, conveniently leaving out my excitement about the agents. I'm trying not to think about it, especially now with his big promotion. I know now that there's no chance he will make a move. I just want to enjoy our night and being together. And what a night it is! Everything is perfect from the food to the company, that is until Kyle asks me something I'm definitely not expecting.

"So, I've been thinking for a while and I wanted to run something by you." He grabs my hand and starts caressing the top of it.

Run something by me? For some reason, my body completely tenses up. I'm sure this isn't a normal reaction for a woman to have when her very dreamy boyfriend is being so sweet.

"What's that?" I whisper. Why am I whispering?

"I wanted to run this by you because I think it would take things to the next level of our relationship." Oh my gosh. My stomach starts to tie up in knots—I'm afraid of what's about to come. "What do you think about us moving in together?" he asks so quickly I can barely make out his words.

What? My eyes open so big I feel like they will pop out of my head.

"Um, move in together?" I ask. "I, I hadn't really thought about it."

I don't really know how else to respond because I really haven't thought about it. I guess it's not a crazy question; it's just so random considering we've never talked about it before. Admittedly, for a brief second,

I thought he might propose. Thankfully he didn't because I know I'm not ready for that.

"I know we haven't ever discussed it. I guess I thought since your parents were moving . . ." He stops. He must notice the shock on my face.

"I mean, if you aren't ready, that's totally okay," he says quickly.

"I don't know," I say finally. "I mean, you know I love you. I just have to think." Ugh, our perfect evening has become totally awkward. This should be an easy decision but there's so much to think about, and it all seems to be moving really fast.

"Oh, you don't have to decide tonight," he adds with a nervous laugh.

I grab his hand. "I promise to think about it and I have to talk to Georgie—I wouldn't want to leave her hanging."

Unfortunately, our date didn't end on as high of a note as it started on. Kyle pretended that he understood, but I could tell that he was disappointed.

When I get home, Georgie is still in her scrubs, eating pancakes on the couch. She makes the most amazing pancakes amongst other things.

"Hey, wow, you look great," she says as she takes another bite of her food. "What's the occasion?"

I tell her all about Kyle's promotion and our perfect date.

"You two are the cutest couple," she says, teasing me.

"Yeah, well, I don't know if he's very happy with me now." I tell her about Kyle asking me to move in with him.

"He asked you to move in with him?" she shrieks. "What did you say?"

She has a look of sheer panic on her face. I have no doubt that she's already trying to figure out what she's going to do if I were to leave.

"Don't worry, I just told him that I would think about it," I say as I get up to get a glass of water.

"So, you're considering it?" she asks worriedly.

"I don't know," I say as I plop down on the couch and lean my head on the back. I'm about to tell Georgie how I've been thinking about moving when her cellphone rings.

"It's Dr. Scott!" she yells excitedly. She clears her throat, fixes her hair, and takes a deep breath. I have no idea why she fixed her hair but whatever.

"Hello," she says calmly as she walks to her room and shuts the door.

I sit there for a few minutes and look around the living room. I think about everything that has happened in the past few weeks. With my parents moving, learning more about my grandmother, and now Kyle asking me to move in with him, I realize I have never been more confused in my life.

# Chapter 5

I really have to start going to bed earlier. Between working on my music and reading Grandma's journal, I have been staying up until the early morning hours. Admittedly, Grandma's journal entries have lost some of their excitement. I'm really tempted to skip ahead, but I don't want to miss a single thing.

Today is a day I've been dreading; I promised my mom I would come over to go through my boxes of stuff. Cassie even called to give me a pep talk; she went on and on about how important it is that we stick together as a family and that we need to support our parents as they spread their wings. Sometimes she's so annoying.

I wish I could call in sick to going to the house. I'm starting to wonder if my attachment is unhealthy? I'm usually not a person who looks at the psychological aspect of things. When I was discussing it with Sophie at the studio the other day, she seemed a little surprised at my devastation to my parents' big move. I guess most people aren't attached to their childhood homes. Granted, I didn't realize I was either until they decided to move.

I finally force myself to get ready. When I arrive, I quietly walk in the door. Sadly, I don't feel like running and sliding on the wood. Maybe it's because I'm not wearing any socks but still.

"Is that you, honey?" Mom calls from somewhere. "I'm in the den."

"Hey, Mom," I say. When I walk in, she is emptying all the contents of the bookshelves into boxes. This is so depressing.

"There you are; I was wondering if you were still coming," she scolds me.

I give her a curious look. Hmmm . . . something looks different. I stand back to get a better look at her. She looks kind of . . . orange?

"Mom, what's wrong with your face?" I ask worriedly.

"What do you think?" she says as she hops off the step stool. She does a little twirl and bats her eyelashes.

"I got one of those spray tans," she says excitedly. "It's about time, right?"

I don't believe it, she did! The woman has lost her mind, or maybe she's having a midlife crisis? Not to mention it's pretty much the worst spray tan I've ever seen. I look at her calves below her navy capri pants and her legs are streaked with orange spray.

"Who did this to you?" I ask in horror. There's no way

she asked for this.

"Sandy's daughter. She spray tanned a few of us after our book club the other night."

I don't know what to say next. I want to be honest but she seems really happy about it, so I'm not sure if it's worth it to hurt her feelings. Luckily, spray tans usually wash off in a few days.

"It looks um . . . good." I lie. "Just to let you know, I have a friend who works at a salon in town, maybe next time you could try her place."

Mom shrugs her shoulders. "Well, maybe, but why pay when I can get it done for free. I have to get ready for beach-living of course." She takes a sip of what looks like one of Cassie's green drink concoctions.

"Your father is coming with me next time to get his spray tan. We will be styling for sure."

I knew it. I should have never gotten out of bed today much less come over here.

"Um, great. So, where are my boxes?"

Mom leads me upstairs to the guest room, which is Cassie's old room. On one side, there are boxes labeled with a C. I can tell Cassie has already started looking through them. On the other side are my boxes. I'm really surprised because there are a lot more boxes than I thought. I guess I better get started.

"So, how is everything going with you?" Mom asks.

"Fine."

"Are you sure? I know the news of the move was hard on you, and I do understand. There are some days that I wish it wasn't happening."

*Then, why are you doing it?* I think to myself.

"I know you may be wondering why we're doing it," she says, reading my thoughts.

"Well . . ."

She grabs my hand.

"It's simple. Because we can," she says with a smile.

That's it . . . because they can? What kind of answer is that?

"So, tell me about Kyle," she says, dropping the whole moving subject. "How are things going with you two? Will I be hearing any big announcements anytime soon?"

Crap! There's no way in hell I'm telling her about Kyle asking me to move in with him. Even this newly spray-tanned version of my mother is still very conservative.

"Not anytime soon. We aren't in a rush," I say as I sit down on the floor. Come to think of it, Kyle and I have barely ever spoken about marriage, maybe once or twice? The idea of marriage would only confuse things even more for me right now.

"I understand that." She agrees. "Well, *when* you two

do start discussing it, I just want you to know that we all really like Kyle. So, we would be thrilled to have him as a son-in-law." That's no surprise because this is not the first time my mother has said this.

When she leaves to get us some drinks, I start looking through the first box. This is awesome; I feel like I'm traveling back in time to the 90s. I find a shoebox full of old Wet 'N Wild makeup (gross) and a half-used bottle of Debbie Gibson's Electric Youth perfume. I'm careful not to spray that because, honestly, I have no idea what it would smell like after so many years. I think that was actually Mom's and she gave it to Cassie and I to play with, making it even older than I thought. The coolest thing I find is a whole bag of cassette tapes, including Madonna, Shania Twain, and Janet Jackson. I remember standing on my bed with a hairbrush and belting out songs for hours. I owe a lot of my passion to listening to these amazing artists.

At the bottom of one of the boxes, I find a stack of songbooks. These will definitely come in handy for my students.

"Did you find anything to sell?" Mom asks after she finally comes back with drinks.

"A few things," I say, pointing to a very small pile. "A lot of garbage and lots of things
  I want to keep."

"Oh, honey, your songbooks," she says, picking one up. "I remember you made me drive all over the city to find some of these. You've always loved your music." She smiles thoughtfully.

I smile at that memory. I remember begging her for days to find the book that had every song from *Annie*.

"Do you ever wish that you had pursued your singing career?"

Well, that question came out of left field. I wonder if Cassie opened her big mouth and told her about our recent conversation.

"Why do you ask?" I'm trying to act nonchalant but she's always been pretty good at seeing through my acts.

"No reason really. All this stuff just brings back memories, even at a very young age you said you wanted to be a singer." She smiles again as if she's reliving the moments of my childhood.

I don't say anything as I continue to empty boxes. Truthfully, I don't know the answer.

"Anyway, all that matters is that you're happy, and I know you are," she says as she rubs my back.

"Yes. I am."

I'm still looking through boxes when Cassie arrives still in her yoga clothes. She looks as if she just arrived off a beach in the islands.

"Why do you look so relaxed?" I ask.

"I've told you that you need to take some classes, little sister, it would do you a lot of good." I roll my eyes.

"Did you find any good stuff?" She starts looking through my trash pile. "Electric Youth?? I can't believe you still have this." She holds up the bottle to her nose to smell it.

"No, I don't still have it. Technically, Mom and Dad still have it," I say, growing more annoyed with her by the minute. She continues looking through the piles on the floor.

"Cass, did you say anything to Mom about what we talked about the other night? About me thinking about moving to New York?"

She looks up from a pile of T-shirts.

"No. Why? Did Mom say something about it?

I tell her about my conversation with Mom regarding Kyle and then her random question about my performing career.

"It doesn't surprise me that she asked you. She's becoming very in tune with her surroundings. We work on that in my meditation class."

I ask her if it was her advice for Mom to get that horrific spray tan, and of course she denied that. I felt bad when Mom walked in and overheard us laughing about it. Thankfully, Cassie manages to change the subject by finding some old pictures of her and her girlfriends. We laugh for a while about how high they teased their hair, and Cassie cringes at the amount of aerosol hairspray she used. She feels really guilty about her contribution to the hole in the ozone layer.

It turns out that we have a lot of fun looking through our stuff, and Mom makes us her delicious lasagna for dinner. She excitedly shows us pictures of the condo they're looking at. Cassie nudges me to act excited and I do my best to pretend but, with as much fun as we had this afternoon, I'm feeling even sadder than ever.

Before I leave, I tell Mom about my conversation with Beatrice.

"I'm so glad she's doing so well. Mother would be really happy that you're going to see her."

"Were they really that close? I don't remember Grandma ever talking about her."

I want to find out as much as I can about Beatrice before I go over there.

"They were very close at one time. I believe they grew apart as they got older, but they still kept in touch. I don't know exactly what happened between them or if anything did. Sometimes life takes people in different directions."

Hmmm . . . This is more interesting than I thought. Did Grandma and Beatrice have a falling out? If they were as close as they seemed in the journal, then what happened? I feel like I'm going back in time to solve a mystery. Now I really can't wait for Saturday to get here.

~*~*~

"What do you think this means?" Georgie asks as she falls back on my bed. I just arrived home from my parents' house when she practically jumps me as soon as I walk in the door. Apparently, Dr. Scott told her, or at least hinted around, that he wants to date her exclusively. She seems to think there's a deeper meaning to his request.

"I think it means exactly what it sounds like. He wants to just date you and nobody else." She looks at me as if I've said something crazy. "I don't get it, isn't this what you have wanted all along? Dr. Scott is amazing, so what's the problem?"

I start to empty the bag of things I brought home. I proudly unpack my songbooks and add them to my special shelf. My dad had gotten me this amazing bookshelf that hangs above my keyboard. Georgie teases me that it looks like a trophy case that you would find in the lobby of a school.

"Problem? Are you kidding? This is the best thing ever!" she screams as she starts jumping on my bed, she then lays down and covers her face as she screams into my pillow.

I haven't seen her this happy in a long time.

"I don't get you. Why did you even ask me what he meant by that?" I lie down on the bed next to her.

"Because you have that crazy good intuition; as soon as I heard you say it, I knew I could believe it."

I laugh. That makes no sense at all. If I had such great intuition, I would know what to do with my life.

"So, when can we plan it?" she asks eagerly.

"Plan what?" I ask. I was too busy thinking about my own life that I didn't hear a word she just said.

"A double date. With our *boyfriends!*" she exclaims excitedly as she jumps up and dances out of my room.

I lie there for a few minutes thinking about everything that's been happening. Despite my emotional day at my parents' house, it turned out to be fine. I'm really happy for Georgie and I have Kyle. I just need to keep reminding myself how lucky I am. I get up to take a shower and get ready for bed.

# Chapter 6

I can't remember the last time I was this excited. Saturday morning has arrived and today is the day for my lunch with Beatrice. I could hardly sleep thinking about it. Truthfully, I don't even know what I'm so excited about. I've thought about this a lot—I know I'm curious to learn more about Grandma, but maybe down deep I'm hoping for an answer to all my questions. Not that a complete stranger will have them, but perhaps the answer lies within Grandma's past.

At the last minute, I decide not to bring the journal being that I haven't made it all the way through it and you never know what she had written in there. What if she wrote something mean about Beatrice? I would feel terrible! Not only that, I haven't even met her yet and I'm not about to share Grandma's innermost thoughts with a stranger, friend of hers or not.

When I arrive at her cute little house, I sit in my car for a minute and collect my thoughts. I can't just walk in there and ask her to tell me everything she knows. I have a feeling that I'm dealing with an old woman who's a little lonely, otherwise why should she be so eager for me to come over?

Before I have a chance to ring the doorbell, Beatrice opens the door. "My goodness. Maris, come in." Beatrice ushers me in. She leads me into her living room, which is decorated more modern than I expected. I guess I expected a little old lady's living room with floral couches and walls of pictures with mismatched frames and lots of cats. Her home is nothing like that; in fact, it looks more like a picture in a Pier 1 catalog.

"Can I get you something to drink? I just made a pitcher of my famous homemade lemonade." She jumps up before I could give her an answer and out of the blue she pulls out a tray of lemonade and a bowl of mixed nuts.

"Please tell me about yourself, and how is your mother?"

I give her a rundown of Mom and Dad and their moving plans, and thankfully it's the perfect lead-in to my questions.

"My parents moving brings me to why I'm here. While I was looking through boxes at their house, I found a journal that was Grandma's. It's a red leather journal and she wrote inside that you had given it to her." I pause as I wait for her to say something.

"Yes, I remember. I gave it to her because I always told her how important it was to keep record of special events. I'm a bit surprised she actually used it. Maris was not the most organized person. Extremely creative but not organized." She smiles and takes a sip of her lemonade.

"She did use it, and it's been really interesting to read. My mom says she never really talked much about that time of her life. I had no idea she was ever a radio performer in New York City until I found the journal. I've always felt a strong connection to her because I'm also a singer and I, too, have always dreamed of performing in New York. I have to admit I was really excited when I found all this out."

Beatrice nods her head. I need to slow down and give her a chance to talk because I keep rambling.

"Anyway, my mom told me that you may know more about that time of her life and I'm just really curious, so any information you can give would be awesome." I finally stop talking.

"Well." She puts down her glass. "As I told you on the phone, Maris and I met in college. We stayed friends throughout our schooling and ran with the same group of friends. She was very talented, and she always went after what she wanted. I admired that about her, everyone did. I remember giving her that journal for her birthday."

I listen as she continues to talk until she's interrupted by the front door.

"Hi, Gran, I have your lunch," a male voice calls.

"I hope you don't mind, but I ordered lunch for us; believe it or not, I'm a dreadful cook. It's a shock, I know. Eighty-nine years old and I still can't cook a good meal. I do make great lemonade though." She holds up her glass to toast.

"Of course, I don't mind."

"My grandson is such a dear and picked up lunch for us. He helps me out a lot since my daughter doesn't live nearby." She picks up her glass. "Come now, let's eat and we can talk more about Maris. I ordered from a delightful little café; their sandwiches practically melt in your mouth."

I follow her into the kitchen. One room after another, I feel like I'm walking through Pier 1.

"Gran, they apologized that they ran out of the chicken salad and gave you this . . ."

What the . . . ? It can't be. I stand there in complete shock.

"Maris?" he says, dropping the container on the counter.

I don't believe it; it's Trevor from Dr. Scott's charity event.

"Trevor?"

Beatrice stands there looking as confused as I feel. "Trevor, how do you know Maris?" she asks, looking back and forth between us.

Trevor smiles smugly. "What would you say, Maris? We *ran into each other* at an event a few weeks ago, right?"

I scowl.

"Yes, unfortunately, I'm so clumsy that I ran into him and spilled champagne all over him and his very expensive suit. Right, frat boy?" I smile through my gritted teeth.

"It's nice seeing you again, too," he says, ignoring my admission. "Now, how is it that you're standing here in my Gran's kitchen?"

Before I can say anything, Beatrice explains about me contacting her and about her friendship with Grandma.

"So let me get this straight, our grandmothers were friends hundreds of years ago." He raises his eyebrows.

"You watch your mouth young man," Beatrice interrupts. I guess she didn't like the "hundreds of years ago" comment.

He laughs. "You contacted my Gran to learn more about your grandmother. Wow."

"This sure is an interesting coincidence," Beatrice says as she nudges Trevor. I can feel myself turning bright red. That's not a good sign. I wish he would just leave.

As if he was reading my mind, he speaks up. "So, I will leave you ladies to have your lunch." He gives Beatrice a kiss on the cheek. "Love ya, Gran."

"No no no, you should join us," she replies and grabs his arm. "There's plenty of food. You don't mind, do you, Maris?"

I want to shout, "Yes, I do." But instead, I just plaster a huge fake smile on my face and shake my head.

"Well, in that case." He grabs a plate out of the cabinet and starts digging into our lunch. Who does this guy think he is interrupting our lunch? Granted, this is his grandmother's house, but still. I have no doubt that Trevor is her pride and joy and he probably does no wrong in her eyes. He just seems so overly confident and arrogant. I know I'm completely overreacting to him being here, but I was really hoping to learn more about my Grandma. And . . . why does he have to be so attractive? *What's wrong with me?*

"Maris, how is everything going with you?" Trevor asks, clearly trying make things less awkward. "Have you been in touch with Liv? Gran, did you know Maris is a singer?"

"I did," she says, taking a sip of her drink, "and I find it fascinating considering my friend Maris was also."

"That's right," he says, pointing at me with his fork. "I remember you telling me you were named after your grandma."

I nod my head. I have to admit I'm surprised at how much he remembers about our very brief encounter. Beatrice seems very interested in our conversation and keeps hinting around how she thinks things happen for a reason. I'm not exactly sure where she's going with that but I can only guess.

"So, how's Giselle?" I ask sweetly. It's my turn to ask a question.

"Doing great."

He gives a very short answer. I remember before leaving the party that they looked as if they were having a pretty heated discussion.

"Mmmhmm . . . you've met Giselle?" Beatrice asks, sounding surprised. I wonder what Beatrice thinks of Giselle? Not that I would be surprised if she didn't care for her, being that Giselle seems like a miserable human being. Granted, I just met her briefly, so I suppose I shouldn't be so quick to judge her. Maybe she was having a bad day? Or . . . maybe she's just a snotty bitch? I have a feeling it's the latter.

"That reminds me, Gran, Giselle wants to take you shopping for your big birthday."

Beatrice makes a face. "Not this again. Why's there so much damn emphasis on this birthday? So I'm turning ninety—big deal."

"What? Of course, it's a big deal." I interrupt. "Ninety is like . . . the biggest birthday ever and you should be celebrated."

She rolls her eyes and folds her arms. "Fine, then, I already told Katherine that she could give me that big party, but I don't want to go shopping." She looks at Trevor. "So tell miss fancy pants that I appreciate the offer but no thanks."

"Got it," he says in agreement. "You know she was just trying to do something nice."

"Ya-ya," she replies.

"Who's Katherine?" I ask, taking another bite of the most delicious fruit salad I have every tried. I close my eyes because it's amazing.

"My mother," Trevor says at the same time as Beatrice says, "My daughter."

"Honestly, what would I go shopping for anyway?" Beatrice asks, sounding annoyed. "A walker or maybe some Depends underwear?"

Okay, so Beatrice has made it more than clear that she really doesn't like Giselle. Shocker!

"Gran, she wanted to help you pick out something to wear," Trevor says, sounding offended. "She even mentioned taking you to your hair appointment."

Beatrice and Trevor continue their banter about Giselle and the birthday shopping. I sit back in my chair and stay quiet. It's pretty obvious that my lunch date is over. I will have to plan another day when stupid Trevor doesn't crash it. I can't leave fast enough.

"Beatrice, thank you so much for lunch," I say after cleaning up my lunch plates. "Unfortunately, I have some work to do this afternoon, but I would love to come back and visit again soon."

"Oh dear," she says, looking worried. "We didn't finish our conversation; I have plenty more to tell you. When will you be able to come over again?"

I look at Trevor who still looks offended over poor Giselle.

"How about I come pick you up and take you out for lunch or dinner?" I don't want to take a chance on Trevor playing delivery boy again. In fact, I hope to not have any more contact with him ever again.

We make a date for a few weeks out. As I'm leaving, Trevor follows me out to my car. "Hey. Sorry about interrupting your lunch. I really had no idea."

I shrug my shoulders. "No problem. Anyway, nice seeing you again." I hold out my hand.

"You, too," he replies, taking my hand. "Drive safe." He looks like he's about to say something else but he doesn't.

On my drive home, I'm frustrated because that did not go as I expected at all. First, Trevor interrupts us, then he ends up staying the whole time, and the worst part is that I really didn't learn any new information. When I come to a red light, I lean my head on the steering wheel. Why is Trevor so interested in me and my career anyway? I admit I feel a little confused about my disdain for him, or maybe my attraction to him? Either way I obviously have issues.

When I get home, Georgie is doing laundry. She must sense my disappointment as soon as she sees me.

"What's wrong with you?"

I dramatically tell her everything about my day.

"Wait a second." She interrupts me. "Are you telling me that the hot guy from the party that you ran into also happens to be your Grandma's best friend's grandson?"

"Yep."

"You know what this is, right? This is a sign," she exclaims.

"A sign for what?"

"Maris!" she screams. "You know I love you, but sometimes you're clueless when it comes to matters of the heart."

What's she talking about? She sounds like a Hallmark card. I'm not that clueless and it's not like I don't know what she's implying and she couldn't be more wrong.

"Ha! I know what you're thinking and it's completely ridiculous. In case you have forgotten, I have a boyfriend named Kyle, and not only that, Trevor is a conceited frat boy who also happens to have a supermodel girlfriend. That pretty much sums it up."

"I didn't think he was that conceited," Georgie says, shrugging. "He seemed nice, but you sure do seem bothered by him."

I sigh. "Whatever. I'm not bothered one bit and it doesn't matter anyway. It just annoyed me that he interrupted our lunch and completely took over the conversation. Anyway, how are things with Dr. Scott?" I ask, trying to get away from this whole Trevor nonsense.

"So good," she says excitedly. "It's just hard keeping things professional at the hospital being that we haven't told anyone we're exclusive yet."

Georgie has told me some pretty crazy stories about the drama that goes on at work. It sounds like a real-life General Hospital. Sometimes I wonder how any actual work gets done there. I mean, are sheets and bedpans ever changed or is it one big soap opera?

"Everyone knows we're dating, but they think it's casual. There is going to be a lot of disappointed women when they find out." She smiles mischievously.

"So, Dr. Scott is the man at General Hospital," I say and give her a wink.

"Very funny," she says sarcastically. "But, yes, he is."

I laugh.

Kyle left me a message while I was at Beatrice's house. When I call him back, he wants to hear all about our lunch. In my mind, I'm trying to decide if I should tell him about Trevor. Being that I have nothing to hide, there's no reason *not* to tell him.

"Beatrice is awesome; she's feisty and fun. She looks fantastic for being eighty-nine years old." I tell him. "It was really cool meeting her and get this, her grandson brought us lunch and talk about a small world. Do you remember Trevor from Dr. Scott's party?"

"Which one was Trevor?"

"He introduced us to Liv and Tom." I remind him. I can tell he doesn't remember, which is fine because I doubt we will ever see him again. "Anyway, it's not important but it was just a funny coincidence."

"I'm glad you had a good time. Did you learn anything new about your grandma?" he asks.

"Not really since we kept getting interrupted. I'm going to take her to lunch in a few weeks so hopefully then."

"That sounds like a plan. Now for some fun news . . . I have a surprise for you."

A surprise? Hopefully this is a real surprise and not another life-changing request like he thinks we should get a puppy or something.

"I have to attend a few days of training for my new job and I was wondering if you wanted to accompany me, *and* it just happens to be in New York City." I can tell he isn't that excited, but I appreciate his enthusiasm for my sake.

I jump off my bed in excitement. "Are you kidding? Of course, I want to come with you."

"I knew you'd be excited," he says, laughing. "I know how much you love to visit, and I promise to make it a fun trip. I have meetings during the day, but afterwards I'm all yours. Do you think it will be a problem to take off the time at the studio?"

"Problem or not, I won't pass up a free trip to NYC." He gives me the dates and I quickly send messages to Lucy and my students that I will be away for those few days. Thankfully, it's several weeks before the recital, so it won't interfere with our rehearsals.

I can't seem to settle down tonight. I read some more from Grandma's journal. I can tell that the momentum of her writing tapered off for a while. She mentions things going well with her radio shows and there is mention of another few friends but nothing really that interesting. As I lie in bed, I think about my relationship with Kyle. I know he still wants an answer to his big question. Truthfully, as much as I love him, I'm just not ready to move in with him. I don't want to hurt his feelings but I need to be honest. I will just wait until he asks about it. I'm in no hurry to bring up that topic again any time soon.

"Maris, that was a beautiful performance," a voice says from behind me. Suddenly, I'm at the studio and the spotlight is on me. I turn around to see who's there, but with the bright light I can't see who it is.

"Who's there?" I ask. I hold my hand above my eyes to shield the bright light. There's no answer.

"Hello?"

'That was a beautiful performance," the voice repeats. I know I recognize that voice from somewhere.

"Who's there?"

I sit up and find myself still in my bed and realize I was dreaming again. I rub my eyes and lie back down and try to fall asleep, but unfortunately, I'm suddenly wide-awake.

I turn on my bedside lamp and find Grandma's journal still sitting there. I figure I may as well read since I'm awake.

*June 15, 1948*

*I'm afraid I haven't been very consistent with this journal writing. I do believe I have good reason. My radio shows have been so glorious and my supervisor told me that my ratings are one of the best at the station. How superb.*

*I have been dating Charles, who is such a gentleman. He took me on a picnic in Central Park and it was lovely.*

*I was supposed to meet Beatrice for tea today but she cancelled again. I wish I knew what was wrong?*

I turn the page and read on to learn more, but her next several few entries have no mention of Beatrice at all. As my eyes get heavy again, I fall asleep wondering what really happened between Grandma and Beatrice.

# Chapter 7

"I don't understand why we're doing another group performance?" Ash says as she stirs her coffee. "Don't you think we should freshen things up?"

Lucy called another early morning meeting requesting an update of rehearsals. Ash has been extra-opinionated at this meeting, even more so than usual. It's way too early in the morning for her nonsense. Sophie looks at me and rolls her eyes.

"We've been doing a group performance at every recital since I opened this studio," Lucy states. I can tell that she's also annoyed by Ash's comments, which is a nice change from her embracing her as the *teacher's pet*.

"Oh, I know and I think it's been great." She agrees. I let out a very big sigh and lean my head back against the chair. She's such a fake; I just hope that Lucy can see through her act. I know she gets on her nerves, but I also know that she enjoys Ash kissing up to her.

"I was just thinking that maybe we could try something new this year," she says innocently.

Of course, she wants to try something new . . . she does this every year. Last year, she wanted to do some weird futuristic theme. Thankfully, it wasn't well received despite her pushing. I give her credit though, when she feels strongly about something she will give it her all.

I tune out the conversation between Ash and Lucy and start to daydream. I'm already mentally packing for my trip to New York with Kyle. I've made a list of places I have to go, and I may wander into a few studios. If I was to ever make a decision to move, I'm not completely naïve to think I will walk off the street right into a starring role. I know I will need to find a job and a place to live and the list goes on. Anytime I think about all this, my head starts to spin. There's so much to think about.

"Maris, what do you think?" Lucy asks me. I come back to reality and realize everyone's staring at me.

"I'm sorry, what was that?"

"She's not even listening," Ash says rudely. "Really, what's more important than this? Maris, where's your dedication? Where's your heart?"

My dedication? My heart? Who does she think she is questioning how much I care? I try my best to ignore her.

"Lucy, you know I will do whatever is best for the studio and the recital. As always, I support your decisions." I stop and glance at Ash. "I don't need to prove my dedication to this school or my teaching ability, especially to her."

Ash shoots me a dirty look; actually, I'm sure I would be dead if looks could kill. I can tell that Lucy is struggling to make a decision. She firmly believes that the workplace should be serene and happy. She thinks that we should all be best friends and frolic around the campfire holding hands. Well, not literally of course, but something like that. She and Cassie should really get together.

"Okay, Ash, thank you for your input." She reaches over and squeezes her hand. "I'm going to take all suggestions into consideration because this recital has to be the greatest show we've ever had. You know that I've done things a certain way for a long time and it's never failed me. That being said, each of you has an important role in this and I am willing to listen to all of your ideas."

I look at Ash's reaction. The smug look on her face tells me that she thinks she's won. Crap! I wish I wasn't daydreaming. I have to ask Sophie to give me a run-down of what I missed.

I'm notorious for daydreaming during these meetings. About a year ago, while I wasn't listening, I agreed to take on a difficult student and it turned out to be a complete nightmare. Ever since then I've tried my best to never agree to anything without hearing the full story and thinking it through.

Ash has always had an issue with me, I'm pretty sure it comes from Mimi choosing me as her instructor. Her parents had her rehearse with each of us before choosing whom she preferred. When they chose me, Ash was very upset and ever since then she's tried to discredit me with Lucy. At first, I went out of my way to be nice to her but then I finally gave up trying, and I wasn't going to let her affect my career.

"Wait," I interrupt. "I actually think we need to continue to do the group performance after all. It's tradition and it shows unity and when our students come together"—I pause and close my eyes—"there's no greater way to represent Do-Re-Mi Studios. I'm sure the families are expecting and looking forward to it and I know the students are."

When I finish talking, I wait for a response from my co-workers or for Ash to throw her coffee mug at me. Lucy immediately agrees with me and quickly tells Ash that we will be keeping the group performance. To her credit, though, she tells Ash that she would be happy to hear any other ideas she may have.

Following our meeting, I head to my office (actually, it's more like a closet, and not the spacious walk-in kind). Ash follows me in.

"I don't appreciate what you did in there, and I know you did it on purpose." She folds her arms and tries to give me a stare down.

"Did what?" I return her stare. "I really enjoy the group performance and I want to keep it. Despite what you think, the world doesn't revolve around you. I'm sorry to break the news to you." I give her the most sweet and innocent smile I can just to piss her off even more. Later I may regret pushing her buttons, but I will cross that bridge when I come to it.

Ash is about to say something but instead she storms off. A few minutes later, Sophie runs into my closet-office.

"Have I told you lately that you're my hero." She shuts the door behind her. "How amazing was that? I wish I recorded it."

I laugh. "Well, as fun as it was to put Ash in her place, I meant what I said, I really do love the group performance. I have a feeling that we haven't heard the last about this though."

I finally kick her out so I can get some work done or at least get some more vacation planning done. I've been a little frustrated with Kyle because he hasn't really expressed any interest in making plans during our trip. He keeps telling me that we can do *whatever I want to do*. I know he doesn't like the city, but I wish he would at least pretend a little for me.

The last trip we went on together was fishing on the Chesapeake with Kyle's cousin, which was miserable for me because I get seasick and I hate fishing. I was trying to do what all good girlfriends do and embrace my man's interests—yeah, that backfired pretty bad on me especially when I spent most of the time praying to the porcelain god below deck. That was the first and last time I went on one of his fishing trips. Needless to say, I'm hoping for a better experience in New York.

I'm happily searching the best restaurants in New York when I start to think about my lunch with Beatrice. I've been meaning to call her to finalize plans. Despite the unfortunate surprise that Trevor is her grandson, I really enjoyed hanging out with her.

As I'm playing on my computer, I type "Trevor Ericson" in the Facebook search box. I don't consider it stalking if I'm just looking at his profile page. It's not like I'm looking through his pictures or anything. I come across his information and I realize that I know nothing about Trevor. During both of my run-ins with him, we've only talked about me, which was not intentional.

I read his profile: Trevor Ericson—Graduate of NYU, Pi Kappa Alpha, Harvard Law—Lover of Chocolate, Golf, and Cartoons. That is probably the most ideal profile for a guy; some might say almost too good to be true. So, Trevor must be a lawyer or at least he went to law school, and for some reason that doesn't surprise me. His profile also says that he's in a relationship with Giselle Le Bon. Ugh, that just figures—I mean, how cool is her name? I wonder if she's related to Simon Le Bon from Duran Duran? I know that's pretty unlikely, but you never know. Before I know it, I've wasted forty-five minutes on social media or, in other words, a typical morning at the office.

An hour and a half later, I'm finishing up with Mimi's lesson.

"Miss Maris, I've made a decision for the recital," Mimi interrupts. "I would prefer not to sing with the other students. I really feel like this is my chance to show my own talents and I shouldn't have to sing with a bunch of kids." She folds her arms in a very teenager-like manner.

I bite my lip, mostly in an effort to keep from screaming at her since I've been down that road before.

"Mimi, that's really disappointing," I say sadly. "You know how much the other students look up you. They'll be very upset."

She pretends not to hear me because, despite being the typical teenager, I know she really cares about the younger students.

"Sometimes I wonder if you really care about my career," she says. "All these group performances don't really show our talents individually."

I don't know when this all came up but it's obvious that Ash has somehow talked to Mimi and planted some ideas in her head about the recital. I knew that she had issues with me but I didn't think she would stoop so low to bring in one of our students to do her dirty work.

"I'm not sure why you think that, but I can promise you that's not true."

"Whatever." She rolls her eyes. "I gotta go."

She grabs her Michael Kors bag and walks out without a good-bye.

I sigh. Maybe I should just pass her off to Ash and let her deal with the nightmare teenage bad attitude. I know I probably should talk to Lucy and have her contact Mimi's mom because this has the potential to turn into a bigger deal than it has to be.

I make my way to Lucy's office. Our studio is a really cool space; the main room/lobby is bright and open with leather furniture. The individual studios surround the main room. Our offices (actually, Lucy's office and our closets) are down a hallway near the entrance. Lucy's door is cracked open and I knock softly.

"Come in," she calls.

I sit down and explain what just happened with Mimi. Lucy listens intently and I can tell that she's frustrated and has come to the same conclusion that I did.

"I'm not saying that Ash talked to her. It's just very coincidental that Mimi doesn't want to do the group performance right after Ash told us that she didn't want it in the show."

Lucy glances out her window. "It's so unfortunate that you and Ash dislike one another. You could do some amazing work by coming together."

Ha! That would never happen in a million years. Ash has never liked me since she came to the studio.

"I don't dislike her at all," I insist. "You know she has never gotten over the fact that Mimi chose to take lessons with me and I think she's taking another shot at it. It's no secret that Mimi is one of the most talented, if not *the* most talented, student we have here. She has a great future ahead of her and you know that Ash wants to be a part of that future."

Lucy listens intently. She agrees to talk to Ash and ask her to back off. I won't hold my breath since I don't really think that Lucy minds her boldness. In fact, I think there is a part of her that enjoys it and in this case that may be a problem for me. I really respect and admire Lucy; however, I will never kiss up to her to further my career. Ever.

# Chapter 8

When I get home from the studio, I tell Georgie about my day and my never-ending situation with Ash. This isn't the first night I have come home complaining about work and probably won't be the last. I don't feel too bad though considering Georgie has spent many hours giving me the play-by-plays at General Hospital.

"I still don't know how you put up with her. I can't believe that she's trying so hard to ruin things for you," Georgie says.

"There isn't much else that I can do. The fact is that Ash is fantastic with her students and she doesn't seem to have much of an issue with the other instructors. Only me."

"Do you think Lucy will end up giving in to her?" she asks, taking a big spoonful of her Ben and Jerry's Ice Cream. We may not keep our fridge stocked but we always have ice cream.

I shrug my shoulders. "You never know. It seems to

be an ongoing problem and the only way it would go away would be for one of us to leave," I say thoughtfully. "Anyway, that won't be happening, so I guess we just have to continue to coexist." *Unless I leave*, I think to myself.

"I still don't get why her students love her so much," she says, interrupting my thoughts. "Every time I've been around her she seems like a miserable person. You would think the students would need someone upbeat and fun."

I totally agree with everything she's saying, but when she's with her students, she becomes a different person. It's almost like that's the only thing that makes her happy. It's kind of sad actually.

"So, when's the big New York trip?" Georgie asks through her mouthful of ice cream.

As soon as she asks I feel the excitement wash over me. "We go in two weeks, which seems like forever away."

"It will be so romantic," she says excitedly. "New York is such a magical place, and you and Kyle will fall in love all over again on top of the Empire State Building. Then you can take a carriage ride through Central Park and share Frrrozen Hot Chocolate at Serendipity." She closes her eyes; no doubt she's imagining some love scene coming to life. "I can't wait to go to New York with Dr. Scott." Georgie is such a romantic at heart. She loves all those sappy romantic comedies.

I force a smile. "Yeah, maybe."

"What do you mean *maybe*? You mean you aren't planning on doing any of that while you are there?" She sounds completely devastated.

I don't want to disappoint her, so I tell her that we have lots of plans. I'm careful not to go into details about Kyle's lack of enthusiasm about our trip. I'm hopeful that once we are there Kyle will embrace the city and we will fall in love all over again. Who knows, maybe on top of the Empire State Building?

After I reassure Georgie over and over again, I go to my room and pull out Grandma's journal. I haven't been faithfully reading as much as I want to so I skip ahead a bit.

*September 27, 1948*

*I'm so upset right now. I thought friends are supposed to love and support you. Is there such a thing as a real and true friend?*

How cryptic. I wonder if she's talking about Beatrice. I skip ahead but there's no more mention about this friend. She only writes about the radio station and her work experiences. It seems as if her career is taking over her life. I have to meet up with Beatrice again.

First thing the next morning, I call Beatrice. Of course, she doesn't answer, no doubt she's screening her calls again. I start to leave a message.

"Hi, Beatrice. It's Maris, just wanting to resc . . ."

"Hello, Maris?" answers a male voice. I let out a frustrated sigh—Trevor.

"Gran is talking to the lawn guy, apparently they planted the wrong plants and she's giving them hell." He laughs.

"That doesn't surprise me. Please just tell her I called." I'm about to hang up but he keeps talking.

"So, how are you doing?" he asks.

"Doing great. Thanks. I have to go but please have Beatrice call me." I hang up quickly.

I sit there with the phone still in my hand. What the hell is wrong with me? There was no reason for me to be that rude. For some reason, I have a big problem when it comes to Trevor and with no good reason.

My phone rings a minute later. I look and see it's Beatrice calling back.

"Hi, Beatrice," I say cheerfully.

"I'm sorry I missed your call. Can I ask you a question?" I tense up hoping that Trevor didn't mention my shortness with him. I don't want her to read more into it than it is.

"Why is it when you pay for a service and you expect the best work possible, people still can't do things right? I mean, I go to the nursery to pick out the plants and they still bring me some hideously ugly bushes." She continues on giving me the play-by-play of her recent experience with the worst landscaping company in North America (her description, not mine).

"They think they're so clever trying to take advantage

of an old lady. Well, I will show them. I will bring them down, I will bring them down to Chinatown." I let her take her time venting because, after all, she's eighty-nine years old.

"So, how are you, dear?" she asks when she finally calms down. "When would you like to get together again?"

Relief washes over me as she doesn't mention one word about how rude I was to her grandson. We make plans for the following Friday, and I tell her that I will pick her up.

"One more thing, dear, I will need your and your parents' addresses. As you know, my daughter is throwing me this big birthday party and I would love for you all to come. I figure if I must attend this stupid thing I might as well make it fun." I laugh as she continues rambling about the party. "What's the party really about anyway? It's like she's saying, 'Hooray for Mom that she hasn't kicked the bucket yet.'"

I give her our addresses before we hang up. I'm not sure how I will get out of attending this party and it's not because I wouldn't want to be there for Beatrice. It's just that running into Trevor and the miserable Giselle doesn't sound like my idea of a fun night out. But I will make an exception because I have a feeling that Grandma would want me to be there.

~*~*~

"Aren't you at all interested in helping me make plans for this trip?" I ask Kyle. We're sitting on his couch getting ready to watch a movie and I'm harassing him yet again about our New York trip.

"Babe, you know I will be busy most of the time with training," he says as he's fiddling around with the TV remote. "We will go to some great restaurants in the evenings though. My co-workers invited us to join them for dinners, so that should be fun."

Is he trying to tell me that we'll be having dinner with the co-workers every night? So much for our romantic trip together, Georgie's big dreams will be shattered. I don't say anything, but I guess Kyle can see the disappointment on my face.

"What's wrong?" he asks, looking concerned.

"I was just hoping we could spend time together. I understand about your training during the day, but you did say that we would have the evenings with each other." He wraps his arms around me tightly. "I mean, I don't mind going to dinner with your co-workers one night but . . ."

"You're totally right, I'm sorry," he says. "In the evenings, I will be all yours so we can do whatever you want."

I smile because most girls would love to hear their boyfriend say that.

"What about you?" I ask. "Anywhere you would like to go?"

I know I'm making a bigger deal out of this than I should. You would think that I'd be excited to pick and choose everything we do. Truthfully, I want to keep talking about our trip to continue avoiding the whole moving in together thing. Neither of us has brought it up since he asked and I know it's coming. Kyle went out of his way to get all of my favorite snacks tonight and he let me pick the movie, so I'm pretty sure he's expecting some kind of answer. That or he's kissing up for something.

"Thanks for getting me all my favorites." I lean over and kiss him. "Let's start the movie." *That's right, Maris, let's start the movie so we don't have to talk about anything awkward.*

I get a bit nervous when he mentions that he has a question; thankfully, he asks about the recital. Before I know it, I end up unloading everything that's been happening with the studio and Ash. It's no surprise when he's as supportive as ever. Unfortunately, my worry comes true when he follows up our conversation about the recital with the burning question.

"So, I know I told you to take your time but I was just curious if you've thought anymore about us moving in together?" he asks nervously. "I promise I'm not trying to rush you, but I was just wondering."

All of a sudden, he looks so sweet and innocent, which seems crazy considering he's asking me to move in with him. It's not that I'm super old-fashioned or anything, but it just seems like it's too soon. I can't even decide what state I want to live in much less make a decision like this.

"I have thought about it, a lot actually," I tell him as I grab his hand. "And I'm just not sure if I'm ready yet." His face completely falls and I know I owe him an explanation.

"Please don't be upset, let me explain." He nods even though he looks as if he might start crying at any second, which would be crazy because men aren't supposed to be the emotional ones. I can't remember ever seeing Kyle cry before. I think he cried about his promotion but those were happy tears.

"There are a few different reasons actually. First of all, I'm on the apartment lease with Georgie for several months and it would be very wrong of me to move out and leave her hanging. On top of that, with my parents moving, it just seems like a lot of change and you know I'm not great with change."

He nods his head slowly and any trace of potential tears has disappeared. "So, there's no other reason?"

What does he mean by that? His question completely catches me off guard. "Um, no. Of course there's no other reason, what are you talking about?"

Kyle rubs his temples with his fingers. "I'm not sure really. Something just seems off with you lately. I keep telling myself that you're stressed out with work and family; I just hope that's all of it."

Huh. I didn't think I was being so obvious but he must have sensed things were off. I quickly debate with myself if I should tell him about my feelings now that I'm leaning toward staying. It's really not even worth the hassle and I'm not really up for any more questions tonight.

"I just wanted you to know that I love you very much."

He continues. "I thought us moving in together would make things less stressful and make you feel better about your family moving. I know how hard that's been, so I wanted to assure you that no matter what, you still have me."

Wow. It's official that the best boyfriend ever award goes to Kyle and the worst girlfriend ever award goes to me. I lean in to kiss him again.

"I don't deserve you at all." I tell him. "I love you, too, and even though I'm going through some stuff right now that doesn't change any of my feelings. We don't have to live together to prove that to each other. Things are good so there's no reason to change it."

Yes! I feel as if a huge weight has been lifted off my shoulders. Kyle seems to be content with my decision and the rest of our night is amazing. I still feel guilty for even considering the possibility of going to New York and I feel even guiltier that I've kept that from him. I have such an attentive and loving man in my life and I know most women only dream of finding someone like him. Perhaps I don't appreciate how good I have it, but a part of me is afraid that I'm never going to be satisfied if I don't take a chance. There's always the possibility that if I did move that we could stay together. I've never believed that I could be in a long-distance relationship but I guess I could try it. That's if I decide to move, and right now I just don't know.

# Chapter 9

It's really bad to drive when you're as exhausted as I am. Hopefully I don't start drifting into other lanes or get pulled over. Kyle tells me all the time that I'm a drifter when I drive and that's when I'm not surviving on only four hours of sleep.

I was awoken several times by that same dream again. The one where I'm in the studio and someone is telling me that my singing was beautiful. This time the voice had more to say; it told me to never stop dreaming and to never stop singing. I had it two times last night and both times I had a hard time falling back to sleep. The strangest thing is that I can hear the voice so clearly but there's no one there.

Admittedly, it's starting to freak me out a little bit. I've never been one to believe in all that crazy dream-ghost-visitors from the other side stuff—in fact, I usually just try to avoid that type of stuff if I can. When I was younger, I went with Georgie and her family to Daytona Beach in Florida. There's a little town not too far from there that we went to called Cassadaga. It's supposedly a spiritualist town filled with psychics, but there are a lot of stories and myths that surround it. I'm not sure what the true story is. Anyway, I was freaked out from the second we arrived until the second we left. Since then, I get really uncomfortable anytime something like that comes up. Despite these feelings, I've been having a strong impression that there's a message I'm supposed to be taking from these dreams. It may just be all in my head or maybe they are just stress-induced dreams.

Beatrice is ready when I arrive and there's not a trace of Trevor, so that makes me both happy and relieved.

On our ride to the restaurant, Beatrice is updating me on the saga of the lawn care situation. I find it so funny that she curses like a sailor when she feels strongly about something.

"Did you receive the invitation to my *party?*" I can tell she's still not excited about this birthday by the way she practically spits out the word *party.*

"Not yet," I reply. "It's really sweet of you to invite me though. I hope you didn't feel obligated."

I don't want her to think that I don't want to go because that's not exactly true even though the idea of spending an evening with the power couple, Trevor and Giselle, is not that high on my list of things to do.

"Of course not!" she exclaims. "I hear it's going to be quite the party, I just wish I didn't have to go."

I laugh. "Beatrice, can I ask you why you're so against this party? I mean, it sounds like your family is just trying to celebrate such a special milestone."

"Yeah, yeah." She rolls her eyes. "Honestly, my daughter just loves to throw a party any chance she can." Hmm . . . that's interesting. I sense some kind of tension surrounding Beatrice and her daughter.

"Come on, I'm sure she wants to celebrate your ninetieth."

"It's not just because of my birthday . . ." she trails off. "I'm sorry, dear, I love my daughter very much, except sometimes we don't see eye to eye. Katherine was always more of a daddy's girl, if you know what I mean, and since my husband passed away, she tries very hard to make up for that and she really shouldn't. The problem is that she goes overboard by treating me like a child. Like this big birthday party for example, you wouldn't believe what she has planned." Beatrice shakes her head at the thought.

"Don't get mad at me for saying this, especially because it's none of my business, but your daughter is obviously proud of you and wants to do this for you. Why not let her?" I lean away just in case she slaps me. She's a feisty old lady so you never know.

"That's something that Charles would say," she says, looking out the window. "They had such a special bond. We were both so devastated when we lost him."

Mayday! Mayday! Things just got really depressing really fast. I need to lighten things up a bit.

"I'm sorry, Beatrice. We can talk about something else if you want," I say.

"Oh no, dear, it's fine." She waves her hand at me. "I don't mind talking about this. We have to talk about our loved ones when they pass, that's how we keep memories alive. After all, that's why we are having lunch together—to talk about Maris."

Yes! I've been so busy listening to her story that I almost forgot about that.

"I apologize again, by the way, that my grandson interrupted our lunch. It's not really his fault, though, because he has strict instructions from his mother to keep a good eye on me. He's a good boy though—always going out of his way for me."

Ha! She called Trevor a boy as if he was sweet and innocent. Although, I can see how much he loves her, so I guess he can't be all that bad.

"He said to tell you hello, by the way." The tone of her voice changes slightly as she smiles.

"Oh yes, tell him hello for me, too," I say quickly. *Seriously, Maris, that was extremely fake and obvious.*

"Can I tell you a secret?" she whispers. I don't know why she's whispering because we're the only two people in the car but whatever.

"Um, sure," I whisper back. Great, now I'm whispering, too.

"I think my grandson likes you; he just doesn't know it yet."

My heart sinks and suddenly I feel carsick. I didn't

know you could get carsick when you're driving.

"Beatrice, you're so funny. I happen to know that Trevor has a girlfriend whom he adores," I say nervously.

"Nah—their relationship will never last," she says confidently. "That Giselle is so full of herself, Trevor will get tired of it. You just watch."

I don't want to watch because I don't care. My grip gets firmer on the steering wheel.

"What do you think of him?" she asks, making me even more uncomfortable. I swallow hard and put on my best performance face.

"Seems like a nice guy and he's obviously devoted to you, which is very sweet." I smile warmly at her. "Honestly, though, I have a wonderful boyfriend, so I don't really think of Trevor in that way."

Beatrice smiles out the window. "If there's anything I've learned in my almost ninety years, it's that you never know the path that your life is going to take. Things happen that bring people into your life for a reason. Sometimes things are meant to be no matter what you expect or plan on."

I'm not really sure what she's implying, although it sure is obvious that she doesn't like Giselle and she's hoping for her grandson to find someone else.

"Don't you think it's curious how you and Trevor met at that party and then again at my house? There's something to be said about that. In fact, that's kind of how Charles and I found each other . . ." All of a sudden, she stops talking and gets a worried look on her face. "Oh, never mind all of that."

She becomes silent, and for some reason the mood has turned very awkward. I'm not sure what has happened, but I can't wait to get out of this car.

When we arrive at the restaurant, she's talking a mile a minute again. We have a great time and she tells me a few more stories about her and Grandma in college. I listen intently, but for some reason I have a feeling that she's leaving something out. It was really odd the way she suddenly stopped talking earlier. I don't want to pry, but now I'm almost convinced that it has something to do with that entry in Grandma's journal. Whatever it is that happened, Beatrice doesn't want to talk about it.

After I drop her off at home, I think about everything. I don't even know why I'm so curious about all of this. Really, why do I care so much?

When I get home, I take out the journal and skim through the pages I've read, looking for some more clues to this mystery. As I read back through, something catches my eye from her June 15 entry:

*I have been dating Charles, who is such a gentleman. He took me on a picnic in Central Park and it was so lovely.*

*I was supposed to meet Beatrice for tea today but she cancelled again. I wish I knew what was wrong?*

Charles? Hold on, didn't Beatrice say her husband's

name was Charles? They have to be different people, right? I skim through the next several entries and there's only one more mention of him, and then nothing. So, did Beatrice steal Grandma's boyfriend? Is that why they had a falling out? That has to be why Grandma wrote about not having true friends.

"Wow," I say out loud.

"Wow, what?" Georgie says from my bedroom door.

"Ahhhh!" I scream as she scares me to death.

"What are you doing?" She's staring at me as if I've lost it.

"Nothing. Just talking to myself as always." I slide the journal under my pillow.

"Okay," she says not even questioning me. "Get dressed because we're going out tonight." She raises her eyebrows and hurries to her room.

I yell out to her that I'm tired, but I'm too late because I already hear the shower running. I guess I'm going out.

~*~*~

Kyle was as understanding as ever when I called and told him that Georgie wanted a girls' night out. All I know is we're going to some upscale restaurant opening with a few of her nurse friends/doctors' girlfriends. This new relationship of hers is definitely putting us on the social scene. I feel like I've become a VIP overnight.

"So, remember when we went to that amazing rooftop party?" she says excitedly. "You know the one where you spilled the champagne on that hot guy that you hate."

I give her a dirty look. She knows damn well that I remember that party.

"Of course, I do."

"Well, I heard that Liv will be joining us tonight, so I thought it would give you more time to chat with her," she says proudly.

I love Georgie! She's that friend who always has your back.

"Really?" I ask. "Don't take this wrong but what's Liv doing hanging with a bunch of nurses?" I say as I wink at her. I didn't mean it as bad as it sounds but I know she won't be upset.

"Yes, well, she probably wouldn't normally hang out with us, but you forget that we're dating the men that her husband is friends with, so I guess that auto-matically makes us cool." She laughs. "And she seemed really nice, so I guess that's a good sign.

According to Georgie, her good friend Hayley from work also happens to be friends with Liv and was invited to this restaurant opening. When she invited Georgie, Georgie asked if I could join them. I guess it really does pay to have friends in high places.

When we arrive, our names are already on the VIP list, how cool is that? Hayley is waiting for us and leads us to a table with six chairs. We stand around talking while we wait for the others to arrive. I don't know why I didn't think about it before but when Liv arrives my heart sinks. There in all her supermodel glory is the one and only Giselle. Liv is talking really fast trying to introduce everyone, and I can see why everyone is drawn to her. It could be because she's really friendly but most likely it's because she's totally VIP. I admire her for the fact that she's a musician, not because she's wealthy or whom she knows, and no matter what, I've never been one to kiss anyone's ass because they're considered important.

"Maris! It's good to see you. I've been expecting a call from you." She air kisses both my cheeks. Was I supposed to contact her? I don't even remember anymore.

"I mentioned you to my friend Miranda, she says she will keep an eye out for your students at the performance."

Miranda, Miranda, Miranda. I need to remember that name.

"That's so nice of you. Thank you." I gush. Hopefully I'm not being over-the-top. I don't want to come across as a phony or a kiss up.

When introductions are made, I still can't understand how Liv could be friends with Giselle. The other girl that has joined us is Candace. She's obviously good friends with Liv also, and maybe it's just me, but Giselle just doesn't fit in with them.

When we finally sit down, I don't say much at first, as

I'm too busy observing. Georgie is to the right of me, then Hayley, Candace, Giselle, and Liv on my left.

"So, how did you all meet?" I ask cheerfully. I'm dying to hear the who's who biography of this crowd. With the exception of Giselle, they all seem very friendly and I feel very comfortable.

Candace is the first to speak up. "My fiancé, Will, Tom, and Sean are good friends. Sean is Hayley's boyfriend," she says, pointing to Hayley. "Sean and Dr. Scott work together at the hospital. And Tom and Trevor went to college together." I can feel my blood pressure rise at the mention of Trevor's name but try not to show any reaction. I can see Georgie glance at me and raise her eyebrows.

"So, when the men started spending long Saturdays playing golf, us girls met up and started having our own fun," Liv adds.

"And now Maris's boyfriend, Kyle, is joining the party," Georgie says as she puts her hand on my shoulder. "Dr. Scott is taking him out to golf with the boys, so he's officially joining their clique."

I glance at Giselle who hasn't really looked up from her phone to join in the conversation. Georgie and Hayley start telling some great stories from the hospital and have us all on the edge of our seats.

As soon as I think Giselle will be silent the entire evening, she finally looks up from her phone and speaks—to me. "So, Maris, I hear that you've become best friends with my boyfriend's grandmother." I look around me as if she's talking to someone else.

"Um, what?" I reply. I sound like an idiot, but in my defense, I'm shocked that she spoke to me and I don't know how to respond to her. I can't get a read on her, especially because I don't know if she was being sarcastic. Maybe she's bothered by the fact that Beatrice and I have spent time together? I figure that she's smart enough to figure out that Beatrice doesn't think very highly of her . . . or maybe not?

"I wouldn't say we're best friends, but we do have a connection being that she and my grandmother were very close friends."

"Well, this sounds intriguing," Liv interrupts. "I would love to hear this story."

I decide to tell them about how I wanted to find out more about Grandma and learned about Beatrice. I'm careful to leave out details in the journal about Charles and a possible falling out. I'm even more careful to leave out anything that has to do with Trevor. I don't need anyone to think that my relationship with Beatrice has anything to do with Trevor. I already suspect that Giselle resents me because of the night that we all met at Liv's party.

"So, the night we met at the benefit you didn't know that Trevor's grandmother was your grandmother's friend? Wow," Liv exclaims.

"No. I actually didn't find out until I was having lunch at her home. Beatrice is awesome though. You would never suspect that she's turning ninety." Giselle looks up from her phone again. I must say something to spark her interest because all of a sudden she's ready to talk.

"Beatrice is fabulous. We've been very busy planning her birthday party. You should try to stop by for a few minutes, I'm sure she'd love it," she says smugly.

Oh, how I wish I could blow her out of the water by telling her how Beatrice really can't stand her, but it would probably be better if I just minded my own business.

"Yes, she told me about it. I'm going to try my best to attend." I smile.

"I would like to make a toast," Liv interrupts, holding up her wine glass. "To new friends and old friends."

"Cheers!" everyone says in unison.

I glance at Georgie who raises her eyebrows at me again. I can read her like a book and I know she's going to have something to say about our conversation. I guess it did sound a little bit like we were fighting over Beatrice, which was definitely not my intention. However, I did need to clear up the connection before anyone got any wild ideas. It just takes one false rumor to cause a huge disaster.

I'm so relieved when Liv starts asking me about the recital. Finally, a conversation I feel like I can enjoy.

The night actually turned out to be very enjoyable other than the brief awkwardness with Giselle. Sure enough, I knew what was coming when Georgie brings up our conversation on the way home.

"That Giselle is a piece of work," she says. "Did you catch on to what she was doing? I mean, the comment about you and her boyfriend's grandma being *best friends*. She's so jealous she can't see straight." She gives a wicked laugh.

"I guess?" I shrug my shoulders. "Apparently she's been trying to take Beatrice shopping and to get her hair done. I think that Beatrice has used every excuse in the book to get out of going places with her."

"See, it's jealousy for sure," she exclaims. "She can't stand that you spend time with her."

I shake my head. I'm starting to feel a little guilty because I'm not purposely trying to make her jealous. I sincerely like Beatrice and it's just another way to feel closer to Grandma.

"Oh well. It's not like I have plans to see Beatrice on a regular basis, and I'm not even sure I'm going to her birthday party."

"Why? You should go. I mean, the woman's turning ninety. Who knows . . ." She stops before she says something about her dying. "Anyway, I'm just saying that you should go."

Sometimes I hate it when she's right.

# Chapter 10

I'm dying to find out if the Charles from the journal is the same Charles that's Beatrice's husband. I have tried to figure out every possible way to approach the subject with Beatrice. I even called my mom and asked her if she has any knowledge about Grandma's boyfriend, and of course she has no idea. I make the mistake of asking her if she knew anything about her mother, and she got mad and hung up on me. I guess I offended her.

I called her back to apologize but it was too little too late. I'm sure the silent treatment will last several weeks, you never know with her. Unfortunately, I've been down this road before. I'm expecting a phone call from Cassie at any time to try to encourage us to make up.

"Hellooo, Miss Maris?" Sadie sings, waving her hand in front of my face. We're finishing her lesson, and once again I'm daydreaming.

"I'm sorry I wasn't paying attention. Great job today!"

I hold my hand up to give her a high five. "Are you getting excited for the recital?"

Sadie nods her head quickly. She starts talking so fast about the recital that she doesn't realize what she's saying.

"I'm just sad about Mimi. I don't know why she doesn't want to sing with us."

I try to make her feel better, but I'm just as disappointed as she is. "It's not that she doesn't want to sing with you . . . she's just really busy." I don't know what else to say.

"Yeah. She's too busy with all her new songs. She says Miss Ash makes her practice extra long." I stand there in shock as I wonder if I heard her correctly.

"What did Mimi say about Miss Ash?" I try to be careful when I ask her because I don't want her to feel like she's in trouble or that I'm fishing for information but of course I totally am.

"She said Miss Ash makes her practice even more than you. That's a lot."

I don't believe this. She's been rehearsing with Ash on the side. I try not to show my anger, especially in front of Sadie. Thankfully her mom arrives just in time before I lose my temper. I quickly rush them out and run to Ash's closet-office, but of course she's not there. I can feel my blood pressure rising by the second. I can't believe that she would actually have the nerve to go behind my back and recruit one of my students. Not to mention that Lucy has strict rules about this kind of thing. It's kind of an unspoken courtesy. She gives all students and their families a choice of which instructor they want to work with. Mimi's family had originally picked me. I have no idea what's happening right now.

I knock on Lucy's door. She's on the phone, so she waves me in to sit down. I practically run in and sit on the edge of the chair. My knees are bouncing up and down so fast I can't make them stop. Lucy must not notice because she continues her conversation. I'm so fired up I contemplate grabbing the phone out of her hand but that probably won't help my case at all.

"What's happening?" she asks when she finally hangs up. I take a deep breath and tell her everything that Sadie told me about Mimi and Ash. Her expression changes but she doesn't seem as angry as I expected she would be. I get the impression that she's not surprised. I'm trying to keep my cool because I have a feeling that I'm not going to be happy about what she's about to tell me.

"Maris, just hear me out before you get upset," she asks calmly. It's a little too late for that.

"Okay," I say through my gritted teeth.

"Mimi and her mother came to me about the group performance. While we were talking, Mimi mentioned that Ash had approached her." She shifts around in her seat. "Let me just say that they love you and she still wants to work with you, she just wants to work with Ash, too."

I look down at my hands. What am I supposed to say

now? I would sound like the biggest spoiled brat if I complain about not getting my way but that's too bad. I've never been known to not speak my mind, especially when I feel strongly about something.

"Well, I respect their decision but I hope you understand how I feel about this. I feel blindsided. I just wish I was told." I look out the window as I wait for her response. "Did you know about this when we talked about Mimi?"

"No. I promise that I didn't. I completely understand how you feel and you're right. I was actually planning to pull both you and Ash in to discuss it, I just haven't had a chance," she says softly. "Mimi and Ash had a brief meeting and I can promise you they haven't officially begun their lessons. At least, I don't think they have. We talked about meeting with you first."

Ha! I can guarantee that Ash has started her lessons on the sly. She's a master manipulator and she will spin it anyway she can to come out on top. There's nothing else to say, so I thank Lucy for her time and quickly leave the studio for the day. I'm so frustrated that I hardly remember driving home. That really freaks me out, but despite my frustration I'm hoping that packing for my New York trip will make me feel better and take my mind off all this.

I start to think about my last visit to New York. Georgie and I spent a long weekend there right before Christmas three years ago. We did the typical touristy stuff and of course we caught a few shows. I have to admit there's nothing more magical than New York City at Christmas. Anyway, we had a great time and I can't wait to experience it all with my man.

My mood has improved immensely, and when I get a call from Cassie I don't even hesitate to answer it. I knew it wouldn't be long before I heard from her.

"First of all, you and Mom are being silly," she says firmly. "You two just need to make up." Really? I guess Cassie has taken on the mother role here.

"This is ridiculous; I'm not mad at Mom. She's the one who hung up on me."

"Enough about that. Tell me about this Beatrice lady. So, she was Grandma's best friend? Why is it that we never heard about her?"

I explain everything that I've learned about Grandma and Beatrice so far. I wasn't sure if I should let her in on the mystery of a possible love triangle between Beatrice, Charles, and Grandma. Although I should probably tell her because Cassie is so in tune with everything that she will know what to do and how to find out more. I tell her all about Beatrice but I carefully leave out anything and everything about Trevor. He has nothing to do with this anyway.

"I did learn something really interesting though," I say. "I have a feeling that Grandma and Beatrice had some kind of falling out. Grandma wrote about dating a man named Charles, then she mentioned something about friends letting her down." I stop because I just remembered that Cassie might not know I still have the journal. I hope she doesn't ask for it.

"And what else?" she asks eagerly. Okay, so maybe she doesn't care about the journal after all.

"Well, when I was talking to Beatrice, she started talking about her husband, Charles, and then she got really quiet. It was almost as if she was hiding something."

Cassie doesn't say anything. "Cass, you there?"

"Okay, so it sounds like Beatrice ended up marrying Grandma's boyfriend. That would make sense as to why Grandma never mentioned her that much."

"Maybe, or it could be a coincidence that their names were both Charles."

I already know what Cassie thinks, the same thing that I do. Beatrice and Charles ended up together which caused a rift in their friendship. Maybe I should just mind my own business and stay out of it. I don't even know if it's worth bringing up something that happened more than sixty years ago.

"It was absolutely NOT a coincidence. Why else would she act so strange?" she replies. "It all makes complete sense. Maris, do you see what's happening here?" Here comes guru Cassie with some kind of deep message.

"For some reason, this was all meant to happen. It's as if Grandma led you to Beatrice."

I don't disagree with her because I do believe I was meant to find that journal, to follow Grandma's inspiration, and not give up on my performing. Although, now I'm starting to feel uneasy, especially after the conversation Beatrice and I had about Trevor. She thinks I was meant to find her because of him.

"Maybe."

"There's no maybe about it, little sister," she interrupts. "You're the connection to mend this friendship. You have to fulfill this task, so you need to ask her about Charles. I really think Grandma would want you to. She obviously got over it because she was madly in love with Gramps. She probably just never got around to talking it out with Beatrice and that's where you come in." That's a lot of pressure.

"Cassie, what should I do? Should I just come out and ask her if she stole her best friend's man and married him?" Seriously, I feel like I'm stuck on some trashy talk show.

"Of course, you shouldn't do that." I can almost see her rolling her eyes through the phone. "She obviously really enjoys spending time with you and Mom told me we're all invited to her birthday party. I definitely won't be missing that party." Okay, I guess my whole family's attending this party now. Perfect.

"You just need to continue to visit her and build her trust."

I feel so overwhelmed. Is Cassie right? Is there a deeper meaning to all of this? Was I meant to find the journal to repair an age-old heartache? Was it to lead me to move forward in following my own dreams or is there some other reason?

I wish I knew.

After I get off the phone with Cassie, I call my mom and apologize for accusing her of not really knowing her mother. I listen to her tell me all about the grandmother we all knew and loved. I think it makes her feel better. It's really not her fault that Grandma kept this period in her life a secret. At least now we can get to know her a little better.

~*~*~

"How excited are you? Don't forget to bring me back some of those rainbow cookies." Georgie is hanging out in my room as I'm getting ready to leave. The day has finally arrived for our New York trip.

"I promise you I will bring you some," I reply for the hundredth time.

"Text me if you can, I want to hear all the details," she begs.

This trip could not have come at a better time. Things have been really tense at the studio and I think a few days away will be good for everyone. Lucy finally had Ash and I sit down together to hash things out and it wasn't pretty. Ash basically accused me of forcing Mimi to choose me to be her instructor. She even had the audacity to accuse me of bribing her. Things got really heated when I reminded them of when she stole some of my material.

"Really, Maris? I thought we moved on from that," she yells. "You talk a big game but you really are full of it." She folds her arms like a spoiled child.

"We did move on from it," I reply calmly. "That is until you went behind my back and put ideas in my student's head. Mimi has always loved doing routines with the other students and they adore her. Now, all of a sudden, she doesn't want to be a part of that. Coincidentally, this all goes down right after you tell Lucy to axe the group performance."

She continues to deny that she put any ideas in her head. Of course, we didn't really get anything resolved and yet again we agreed to coexist. I don't know how much more I can take. Poor Lucy is stuck in the middle and I feel bad about that, but I don't know what else can be done.

"Oh wow!" Georgie yells from the living room. "There's a big fancy car outside. That must be for you." I think she's even more excited about this trip than I am.

"Yeah, Kyle's company sent a car to pick us up."

"Have fun!" She gives me a hug and I walk out to meet Kyle, who's holding the door open for me.

"You ready?" he asks, kissing me on the cheek.

"Ready for New York? Always."

# Chapter 11

*You really can't get any better than a luxury hotel overlooking Central Park*, I think as I look out my window. I'm still lying in bed waiting on my breakfast to arrive from room service. Kyle left very early for his training, so I'm on my own for the day. We've been in New York for less than twenty-four hours and so far I'm having a really good time.

After we arrived, we met up with some of Kyle's partners and their wives for dinner. He's by far the youngest of the partners, but we had fun even though it felt like we were hanging out with our parents. Kyle promised me that this would be the only night we would do a work dinner. Today, I'm going shopping and I got up the courage to text Liv and ask for Miranda's contact information. Thankfully, she texted right back and also offered to let her know that I may be contacting her. I admit that there's a small part of me that wants to brag at the studio if I actually get to meet with an agent who will be attending the recital. I'm sure that will get Ash fired up and I really don't care.

When I'm finally ready, I take off on my adventure in the city. As soon as I walk out onto the street I feel this sudden exhilaration. Honestly, I could get used to this scenery every day. I take my time as I head toward 5$^{th}$ Avenue; I have no doubt that I'm walking slower than everyone else in this city and I don't care. My phone starts buzzing; I'm hoping it's a message from Liv telling me that she spoke to Miranda but it's not, it's a text from Georgie.

How is it?

I'm actually surprised it took her this long to text me.

Fine. Just got here. Heading to 5$^{th}$ Ave. Jealous?

Georgie loves 5$^{th}$ Avenue, so I already know what her answer will be.

Of course! No fair.

I laugh as I continue my stroll, walking past Tiffany & Co. This store totally reminds me of that movie *Sweet Home Alabama* where Reese Witherspoon's boyfriend proposes in the store and tells her to choose any ring she wants. That has to be one of the best scenes from a movie ever. I really could see Kyle doing something romantic like that, not in New York of course, but he is sweet enough to pull off a big surprise like that. Not that I want him to propose anytime soon, but if that were ever to happen it would be something very creative I'm sure.

A few hours later, I'm sitting in Starbucks enjoying my decaf Caramel Macchiato and people watching when I get a text from Liv.

Miranda is expecting your call.

I feel like I may be imagining what I read.

Wow. I will reach out to her. Thank you so much.

Now that I have this opportunity, I don't know what to say exactly when I call her. Should I tell her about my students or should I mention my own career? Considering that I'm not very happy with Mimi right now, she doesn't deserve for me to go out of my way for her. In fact, the vindictive part of me almost wants to hand her over to Ash especially after what they've done to me. I pull out my phone and make some notes for my phone call. I'm really nervous all of a sudden, which is absolutely crazy because this isn't the first time I've spoken with someone so connected in this industry.

I call Miranda and she answers immediately. She's really nice, but I can tell that she's really busy or preoccupied with something. We make plans to meet for coffee on the last day I'm in New York, which is still a few days away. At least that will give me some time to think about what it is that I'm hoping to accomplish with this meeting because I really don't know.

When I finally get back to the hotel, Kyle is not back yet. I take a hot bath and wait to hear from him.

I get another call from Georgie.

"Checking up on me already? I just barely got back

from my adventure on Fifth Avenue."

"Ha! You don't have to rub it in," she snaps. "Actually, I'm calling to tell you that you got some very important mail today. The envelope is huge and I was wondering if you wanted me to open it?"

In translation, she wants to open it because she's super nosy.

"You can open it, go ahead."

"Okay," she says eagerly. I can hear the rustling as she opens the envelope.

"Well, isn't this fancy," she says.

She reads: "Your presence is requested to join in celebration of Beatrice's Ninetieth Birthday. Saturday, June eighteen at six p.m. at the Hyatt Regency Hotel and Spa. Please use the enclosed response card to confirm or decline your attendance."

"Thanks. I will have to check my calendar when I get home."

"You mean you're still not sure if you're going to go? I will gladly go in your place. This sounds like it will be an amazing party." She asks, "Be honest with me, what's really going on?"

Just then Kyle walks in. Yes, I'm saved.

"Hey, Kyle just got back. Can I call you later?"

She knows I have no intention of calling her back

tonight.

"Ohhhhh yeah, have fun tonight."

Kyle has already laid down on the bed and he looks like he's about to fall asleep. This isn't looking very promising for a night out on the town.

"How were your meetings?" I ask.

"Good," he replies. His face is in the pillow. I walk into the bathroom and continue to get ready because I'm going out tonight with or without him. I take my time doing my hair and makeup, giving him a few minutes to get a power nap. When I finish getting ready, I stand in front of the mirror, checking myself out. Here goes . . .

"Kyle, wake up!"

# Chapter 12

The next morning I get up early and go to the gym in the hotel. I haven't been to the gym in months, so I guess this makes me one of those people who only exercises while on vacation but never in day-to-day life. While I'm walking on the treadmill, I think about the events of last night. When I finally got Kyle to wake up from his nap, we ended up going to Gramercy Tavern for dinner and drinks and I managed to get him to take a carriage ride through the park, which was pretty romantic. It was a nice evening even though I don't think he really felt like going out. Again, he made it really obvious that he has no interest in enjoying the city. He was as sweet as ever to me but he would be that way no matter where we were.

Anyway, today I have plans to pop into some studios to hopefully make some contacts, and tomorrow I have my meeting with Miranda. When Kyle asked what my plans were, I told him I was going sightseeing. I don't consider that lying exactly. I just didn't feel the need to give him specific details.

After my very overdue trip to the gym, I get a text from Cassie. My heart sinks as I read it.

The house has two offers, just wanted you to know. Love you.

Wow, that didn't take very long. I guess this is all really happening and there is nothing I can do about it. Throwing a tantrum or complaining about it isn't going to change anything.

Thanks for letting me know.

I text her back and finish getting ready. I have two more days here and I'm going to enjoy myself even if I have to do it alone.

So, despite the text from Cassie in the morning, I had a really good and productive day. I really love productive days. Although I didn't make any contacts, I was able to make lots of notes and I found some studios to contact when and if I finally make a decision. In the meantime, I'm going to enjoy the night with my man.

I look at the clock on the nightstand to see that it's 6:45, and I'm beyond frustrated. Kyle texted me an hour ago and said that he was almost done with meetings for the day. I hope that nothing bad has happened to him. The last thing I need is for him to get mugged or stabbed or something crazy to make him dislike the city even more than he already does.

I tried calling him a few times and his phone goes straight to voicemail. As I'm waiting, I realize that this trip has not been what I was hoping for. I know I had full disclosure that it was mainly a work trip, but at the same time I was hoping for more. As the minutes pass, I grow more and more angry.

At 7:40, Kyle finally rushes into the hotel room.

"I'm really sorry, honey. Jim and Tom stopped me and wanted to discuss a few things and my phone is dead." He shows me his phone. "I will change and be ready in five minutes."

He doesn't really give me a chance to say anything, which is probably the best thing since I'm pretty mad at him. I sit on the edge of the couch, tapping my toe with my arms tightly folded. I could carry out this silent treatment all night if I need to, my mom taught me well.

On the other hand, we only have a few nights left here and I should try to enjoy it as much as possible.

"I'm ready." He hurries out of the bathroom, fixing his hair. "What's the plan? I'm all yours."

I glance out the window and take a breath.

"Where do you want to go?" I ask him.

"I told you anywhere you want."

I don't know what comes over me. It could just be my frustration over Kyle being late or maybe it's a combination of everything.

"I think it's time I told you something," I reply.

His smile turns to a look of worry, so I reach over and

grab his hand.

"There has been something going on with me lately. I thought I could just ignore how I was feeling but I think it's only fair I was honest before I make any decisions."

Kyle sits down slowly on the couch with me. His worried look has turned to fear.

"You can relax, it's nothing too horrible." I reassure him.

I explain everything to him about how I have been struggling with the path I should take for my future. Then I tell him about the moment I found the journal and I learned about Grandma being a radio performer. I tell him how I felt it could be a sign for me to reconsider my plans of following my own dreams. He patiently listens to me without interrupting and rubs my back as I get tears in my eyes.

"I love you and I want to be with you, but I hate feeling like I may regret something if I don't give it a chance." I finally stop talking and wait for him to respond to my confession.

"Why haven't you said anything?" he says. "I knew that something was bothering you. You should have told me how you've been feeling."

"I wanted to but then you got the promotion." I blow my nose loudly into a tissue. "And let's be honest, you've made it more than clear that you have no desire or plan to move here. Then you asked me to move in with you and I was even more confused." I shrug my shoulders.

"You're so amazingly talented," he exclaims. "I think you would be able to continue your career no matter where you lived, so why would you have to be here? We can find you an agent and you can travel when they need you."

I appreciate his confidence in me, but at the same time I realize that he still has no intention of ever moving. I think I'm going to need to make this decision on my own.

"Thanks. I just want you to know that I haven't made a decision yet, but I promise you that I will consider every possibility before I do." I walk to the window and stare out at the view of this city. The city where dreams come true, the city where my grandmother followed her dreams yet she still found love and happiness after her career.

"Are you breaking up with me?" he asks. As sweet and patient as Kyle is, I can sense his frustration.

"No," I say. "Just please understand that I need to figure this out, so please be patient."

"Okay," he says. "I'm really sorry I was late."

I smile. "I know."

Of course, our night has been ruined by my honesty. We ended up ordering room service and quietly watching some horrible made-for-TV movie. We briefly discuss our plans for the next day and I tell him about meeting with Miranda. He wishes me luck and we awkwardly kiss each other good-night.

I have a horrible night's sleep. I lie awake for what feels like hours and I watch the clock every hour on the hour. I drag myself out of bed after Kyle leaves for his meetings.

As I slowly walk to Starbucks, I thought I would be more excited to meet with Miranda but I'm not. In fact, I can't believe I'm saying this but I'm just ready to go home. When I arrive, she's waiting for me.

"Maris, it's fantastic to meet you. I'm Miranda Adams." She holds out her hand to shake mine. Miranda is absolutely stunning and dressed perfectly from head to toe.

"Thank you so much for taking the time to meet me; I know how busy your schedule is."

"Not at all. Livie is one of my dearest friends. I'm happy to do this for her." She takes a sip of her Skinny Vanilla Latte (*I know my Starbucks cups*). "Okay, tell me all about these talented students I've been hearing about."

I'm so glad I met Miranda because having coffee with her has been the best part of my trip. How pathetic is that? Here I am in one of the most exciting cities in the world with the love of my life and the best part of my weekend has been a thirty-minute meeting in Starbucks with a stranger.

I tell her all about the students, including Mimi. No matter how upset and hurt I feel over everything that happened I would never let my feelings of her recent behavior affect her future. I even mention that Mimi is working with both Ash and myself, although admitting that was like stabbing myself in the stomach over and over again.

"Well, it sounds like it'll be a great show and we're always looking for fresh talent." She glances at her phone. "Livie told me that you used to sing as well. Why did you stop?"

Why did I stop? How do I answer this question when I don't even know? I'm starting to wonder how I've gotten to this point. All of sudden I feel anxious— maybe I'm having a panic attack or the start of a midlife crisis? I don't really know what a midlife crisis feels like or at what age you should be to have one.

"Maris?" she interrupts my thought.

"What?" I answer absentmindedly. "I'm sorry. I zoned out for a second."

I'm so embarrassed but thankfully Miranda gets a phone call and excuses herself. In my mind, I rehearse a few "good" answers to her questions.

"I hate to do this but I have to rush out," she says as she hurries back to the table. "So, great meeting you and I look forward to seeing you at the performance, if not before."

She quickly leaves and once again I'm alone in New York. Now I'm definitely ready to go home.

~*~*~

"So, you are telling me that you guys hardly spent any time together? I don't understand."

When Georgie gets off her shift, she immediately demands I tell her about our trip. I've been home for one day and this is the first time we've seen each other. Kyle and I have texted a few times but the awkwardness remains and I hate it. I give Georgie the play-by-play and I didn't realize how bad it was until I have to relive it.

"But, he was willing to do anything you wanted and you got mad at that? I don't understand what's going on with you?"

I close my eyes and hang my head. I could blame it on the possibility of a midlife crisis but I don't think she'll buy that. In my defense, he promised me that we would spend our evenings together—not that he would fall asleep or be two hours late.

"Because I wanted him to be happy to be there and to fall in love with the city so that he would want to go with me if I ever decide to move there. I love Kyle and I want to be with him, but I don't know if we want the same things, at least not right now."

Georgie doesn't respond right away, no doubt she's processing my admission that I'm thinking about moving so I tell her everything.

"Yes, I've been thinking about moving because I don't know what I'm supposed to be doing right now. Things at the studio are not great, my parents are selling their house, and I really miss performing. I just feel like I'm in a rut in my life and I have to do something."

All of a sudden, I think about a few things Grandma wrote in the journal.

"I have to show you something." I make Georgie follow me to my room and I reach under my mattress and pull out the journal.

"I found this in a box at my parents' house, it belonged to my Grandma." I finally hand over the journal after spending weeks keeping it hidden.

After reading several pages, Georgie looks up.

"Wow. This is amazing, and this is how you found out about Beatrice. Very interesting."

I can see the look in her eye. I'm silently praying that she doesn't say a word about Trevor. I don't need her and Beatrice teaming up and complicating things even more than they are.

"Does Kyle know about this? I mean, about what your grandmother did and about you finding this? Maybe you should be honest with him."

"I was honest with him and his answer was that I could find an agent and commute when I was needed. He doesn't grasp that I want to perform in New York. I've always wanted that. But, I want to be with him, too—so, what am I supposed to do?" I feel like I'm begging for someone to give me an answer. But the truth is that neither Georgie nor Cassie can decide this for me. This decision is all mine and I need to make the right one.

# Chapter 13

It's been a little over a week since the New York trip disaster. Thankfully, I've been really busy so I haven't had much time think about it. Lucy has kept our schedules packed with lots of rehearsals, meetings, and costume fittings. Ash and I haven't spoken a word to each other, which has been really nice for me but I know it makes things really uncomfortable for everyone else. I don't care though because this is not my fault and Lucy knows it.

"I wish I knew what we could do to get her out of here," Sophie says in between chomping on her ice from her drink. I really wish she would stop that because it drives me crazy.

"Come on, you know that will never happen. As long as she continues to kiss Lucy's butt, she's staying put."

"Yeah." She takes another mouthful and starts chomping. "So, tell me about your trip. You haven't said anything about it."

I cringe at the thought of having to relive that horrible trip.

Kyle and I've seen each other a few times since then and things seem to be okay. Neither of us has brought up the trip. I figure I need to let things play out until after the recital and then decide what I need to do. Thankfully, he agreed to attend Beatrice's birthday party with me this coming weekend. I've never been less excited to attend a party than I am for this one, but I called her personally to tell her I, along with my whole family, would be attending.

I'm trying to take Cassie's advice and continue to build her trust so I can figure out the whole thing with Charles and Grandma.

"Have you lost weight?" Georgie asks when she sees me in my dress. Saturday has finally arrived and I'm getting ready for the party.

"Yes, I have. Stress will do that to you," I say as I reach for my hairbrush.

"You look really good," she says, sitting down on my bed. "Not that you didn't before." She adds, "Things okay with Kyle?" She and I have been on completely opposite schedules so we haven't spoken much since I came home from New York.

"They seem to be." I shrug. "I guess we will see what happens."

In the mirror, I can see her. She opens her mouth to say something but quickly closes it. I can tell she dying to say something. "What?" I turn around and face her.

"Go ahead and say what you want to say."

She can tell I'm irritated because she shakes her head and tells me to forget it. Of course, that's never going to happen. "You might as well just say it."

"I was just thinking that Trevor would probably be at the party tonight, too . . ." she trails off, giving a look of pure innocence.

I knew it. It's been weeks since I showed her the journal. That may be a new record for her keeping her mouth shut.

"Of course, he'll be at the party; he's Beatrice's grandson, and I'm sure Giselle will be there right by his side. So you can stop with the innocent act." She gives me a smug look and saunters out of my room leaving me completely annoyed.

~*~*~

I hope that if I live to be ninety years old someone throws me a birthday party like this. Or any age for that matter. As soon as I walk in I can see that Beatrice's daughter has gone above and beyond to make this a memorable night. Although I don't see Beatrice, I hope she hasn't snuck out through a bathroom window and made a run for it.

Kyle and I arrive a few minutes before my family, but as soon as they get there Cassie pulls me aside and wants to talk about the Charles/Beatrice/Grandma saga.

"I don't think this is the place to discuss this," I

whisper loudly. A few people standing nearby turn to look at me. Great.

"Maris, I'm so glad you came," Beatrice says. I turn to see her standing there in a floor-length black gown, her neck and ears full of diamonds, and a beautiful pinned corsage. I hope she didn't hear Cassie and me talking.

"Of course." I raise my eyebrows at Cassie. "Happy birthday!" I give her a big hug and introduce Cassie

"Hello, Beatrice, I'm so happy to finally meet you." Cassie holds out her hand and smiles warmly at her.

"Cassie, you're all grown up. I remember when Maris sent pictures of you, your grandmother Maris not this one," she says, pointing at me. "Of course, you were much younger then but you look a lot like her." Cassie smiles as she continues talking.

"This is so nice of all you, it means a lot to have you here, more than you know."

Cassie glances at me and starts to look about the room. I'm sure she's channeling the auras to help us get to the bottom of the mystery.

If she starts chanting, I will pretend like I don't know her. My parents join us and Beatrice seems absolutely overjoyed to see my mom especially. I see Mark and Kyle in a corner, playing on their phones. I don't expect them to move from those spots for most of the evening, which is fine because things are still so weird between Kyle and me. We probably should've just left them home.

"Hey, stranger," a voice whispers in my ear from behind me. My stomach does a backflip and I cringe. I take a deep breath and turn around.

"Hi, Trevor," I reply flatly. Hopefully he doesn't notice my discomfort at seeing him.

"This is quite a party; your mother outdid herself." I figure I might as well try to make conversation. Come to think of it, I realize I still haven't seen his mother yet. I look around and see a stunning woman walking around greeting guests. She's the spitting image of Beatrice, only younger of course.

"Is that your mom?" I ask, pointing in the woman's direction.

"Yes, that's Mom in all her glory. She's been planning this party for months. So far she and Gran are getting along and I haven't had to break up any fights yet." He holds up two fingers crossed. He leans in to whisper something to me, "Trust me when I tell you that you don't want to ever get in a fight with either of them." His warm breath on my neck gives me chills. I subtly move a few inches away. "Thanks so much for coming tonight. Gran was so happy, and I think the fact that you all came has made this party somewhat bearable for her. She kept saying something about life coming full circle. It didn't make much sense but sometimes Gran rambles on."

I wonder what she meant by that? I will tell Cassie and she'll be able to decipher it. "It must have something to do with her and my Grandma. I'm just glad we could be here to celebrate even though she doesn't want to be here. Part of me was wondering if she was going to try to sneak out," I say with a smile.

"Oh believe me, I'm watching her." He winks at me. He points to the drink in my hand. "Oh, and I wanted to thank you for not spilling your drink on me tonight. This is a new jacket and my mom would be really pissed at me if I look the slightest bit disheveled." What a jerk . . . I'm actually tempted to pour it on him anyway.

"Ha-Ha." I scowl and then crack a smile. I look over to see Cassie watching us curiously. Crap! Now I'm going to have to explain how I know Trevor. It's practically impossible to hide anything from her (not that I have anything to hide.). I really believe that she could have superpowers.

"I better make sure my mom doesn't need anything. But I will catch up with you later, and I still need to meet your family."

A feeling of panic comes over me. No, he certainly does NOT need to meet my family. After he walks away, I'm careful to avoid Cassie and her curious stares. I make my way over to where Kyle is still sitting. At least now he has a plate of food.

"You bored?" I ask. He looks up from his phone and shakes his head. Not like Kyle would ever admit if he were bored. Just as I'm about to sit down next to him, Cassie comes over and asks to talk to me in private.

"Can we talk later?" I beg. "I've left my poor date alone in the corner all night." I put my arm around Kyle.

"It will just take a few minutes and Mark will keep him

company. Right, babe?" she asks.

"Yep," Mark says without looking up from his phone. Typical Mark, he usually just goes along with anything Cassie says anyway.

Cassie links her arm in mine and walks me out onto the terrace—drags me out is more like it. I fold my arms and mentally prepare myself for what's about to take place.

"Who was that guy?" she asks before I even have a chance to say a word. "And don't say that he's nobody because clearly he is."

I seriously wonder what I did in a past life to get Cassie for a sister. I feel like I'm in high school again when Cassie would tell our parents anytime I did anything wrong. She was always an overachiever and I just wanted to have fun and sing. Because of her, I got caught skipping school and sneaking out of the house. I've still never forgiven her for telling on me. Now that we're older, she still watches what I'm doing.

"First of all, that *guy* is Beatrice's grandson, Trevor. He was just telling me how happy she was that we were able to come tonight, and he says she kept talking about things coming full circle. Do you think that could have something to do with Grandma and Charles?"

I'm hoping that talking about Beatrice will take Cassie's mind off whatever she thinks she saw while I was talking to Trevor.

"Trevor, huh?" she repeats his name. She obviously

didn't fall for my plan to change the subject. "If he's just Beatrice's grandson, then why did you all seem to know each other so well? It almost seemed as if you've known each other for years or maybe even lifetimes."

Oh, here we go . . . I roll my eyes.

"He brought Beatrice and I lunch the first time I was over there and he ended up staying," I say non-chalantly. "He was there for the majority of the day, so we talked quite a bit. And just so you know, he has a girlfriend."

Which reminds me, I haven't seen the lovely Giselle yet either. Maybe she got sick and couldn't make it? Unfortunately, I'm not that lucky.

"I see that now," she says, looking over my shoulder. I turn around to see Giselle and she just happens to be wearing the tightest and shortest gold dress I have ever seen. Not exactly appropriate for an old lady's birthday party or for anywhere other than maybe the street. She's standing next to Trevor's mother and laughing loudly. She must be drunk because she's totally making a scene. Cassie is still watching her along with most of the guests at the party.

"She's a real piece of work, isn't she?" Beatrice asks when she joins us as we watch Giselle make her way around the room. "I'm waiting for Trevor to kick her out on her ass but no such luck yet." She makes a face.

"My daughter likes her and I have no idea why. But then again, she's always been a bit more trusting than me, which is probably a good thing. She's just like her father; he would give anyone a chance. Not that that's a bad thing, I guess we should all be more like that." She stares off into the distance and Cassie and I exchange looks.

"Your husband sounds like he was a wonderful man," Cassie says. "If you don't mind me asking, when did he pass away?"

"A few years now. He was a good man," she says with a smile. "He was damn annoying though, and he always cheated while playing cards. Most of the time I wanted to smack the shit out of him, but I loved him more than anything."

We all laugh.

"I feel that way about my Mark, too, sometimes. That's him sitting over there in the corner. He and Kyle are playing on their phones and being antisocial." She points to the guys.

"Who's Kyle again?" Beatrice asks. Oh, this could be bad. I'm praying she doesn't say anything about Trevor and me. Not that there's an actual Trevor and me.

"Kyle's my boyfriend, remember I told you about him?" I remind her.

She gets a confused look on her face. I really hope she isn't using this opportunity to be forgetful.

"Yes, I do." She nods her head and looks over at the guys. "He's really handsome . . . but not as handsome as my Trevor."

Okay, I need to find a table to crawl under so I can die

now. I try to avoid all eye contact with Cassie because that's the worst thing I could do at this point.

"Trevor, as in your grandson?" Cassie asks curiously.

*No eye contact, no eye contact, no eye contact,* I chant silently.

"Yes. My sweet Trevor, have you met him yet?" she asks excitedly. "Come on and I will introduce you." She pulls Cassie away, leaving me frozen in my spot. Never mind Beatrice, I think I need to escape through the bathroom window.

As the party continues, I'm now convinced that I am having a midlife crisis because I have absolutely no reason to feel this uncomfortable around Trevor. Every time I see him, I try to move as far away from him as I can. He's never done anything to cause me to dislike him so much. Or maybe that's just it; maybe I don't dislike him at all. As if things couldn't get any worse, Giselle is making her way around the room and coming right toward me. I look around but I have no time to escape.

"Maris, it's very kind of you to *stop by*." She slurs her words. Yep, she's definitely drunk. It might be my imagination but I really think she's glaring at me.

"Thanks. You look nice by the way," I say and smile sweetly. Wow, that actually sounded sincere.

She looks down at her dress and starts to run her hands up and down her sides. "I only picked this dress because Trevor loves it so much."

Of course, Trevor likes that dress considering it's

basically a small piece of fabric that covers her body just enough to not be arrested. I consider making a smart-ass comment but I bite my tongue. I don't need to give her any more reason to dislike me, and I can't forget the fact that she's Liv's friend. I definitely don't want to burn that bridge.

"Don't you think he looks sexy tonight?" she taunts. This conversation is taking a bad turn really fast.

"It's good seeing you," I say, ignoring her question. "I probably should check on my boyfriend." I must have said something very interesting because all of a sudden Giselle's demeanor completely changes.

"Your boyfriend is here? Where?" she asks. I get the feeling that she thinks I'm lying as if I made up some mystery date that doesn't exist.

"He's sitting in the corner with my brother-in-law, probably playing some football game on their phones. My sister and I dragged them here tonight but they're good sports nonetheless."

I quickly escape and check on the guys who are still in the same spot that we left them in. I really need to get some air so I wander out onto the terrace. I look out into the evening sky and think about how I got here. I know Grandma led me to this point because ever since that moment I found her journal things have changed. I can totally be honest with myself and admit that I find Trevor attractive, and yes, it is interesting that I met him just before meeting Beatrice. But . . .

"What are you thinking about, young lady?" Beatrice interrupts my thoughts. I sigh because no matter what

I do I can't get a minute to myself. Maybe I should go hide in the bathroom stall to have a minute of privacy. "I'm hoping you're coming up with a plan to break me out of this place."

I smile at her. "Come on, it's not *that* bad."

"I suppose." She walks over and joins me where I'm looking out into the sky. "Katherine did a nice job and Charles would have loved this. He loved to go to parties and be surrounded by people. No doubt Katherine got her people skills from him."

I stand there and listen. I take a deep breath and ask her the million-dollar question.

"Beatrice, I want to ask you something." Her peaceful smile turns into a worried stare. "What really happened between you and Grandma?"

Silence. But it's more like awkward and uncomfortable silence.

"I was wondering when you were going to ask me that. I can only imagine what Maris wrote in that journal."

I try to reassure her that there really isn't much in there except for that one entry. She must believe me because she's finally ready to talk.

"Maris was popular and she had many suitors. All through school and even after we had our graduation." She pauses and closes her eyes. "One summer evening, a group of us went to Coney Island. It was a lot of fun back then, we would go and eat ice cream and talk about our futures. While we were there, we met a few young men—they were all so very nice and believe me when I tell you that Maris got a lot of attention from them. She was beautiful."

She pauses again and I can tell she's remembering everything that happened that night.

"That's the night I met Charles. I have to tell you that prior to that night I didn't believe in love at first sight, but that all changed. I fell in love with him the moment I saw him."

I get a little emotional as I watch her face change when she talks about Charles because there's a certain vulnerability that she doesn't express at any other time.

"Charles had a friend that worked at the radio station with Maris, they spent a lot of the evening talking but it was mostly about their mutual friends. I admit I was very jealous, especially when they made plans to go out on a date."

I'm listening so intently that I feel like I'm back in 1948 with them.

"I believe they went out a few times, but Maris told me that she wasn't ready to settle down. She was very into her career in those days." She pauses. "Anyway, things kind of fizzled for them within a few weeks. One afternoon, I ran into Charles and we ended up talking for hours. He asked me on a date and I went and we fell in love. The mistake I made was keeping it from Maris, even though she was already dating another man. She felt betrayed and she was very angry with me. I avoided her as much as I could so I could keep it a secret. When she found out . . ." she pauses again.

"Well, things were just never the same."

She opens her clutch purse and pulls out a tissue. She dabs the corners of her eyes.

"I never explained things, and to this day I wonder if she thought I stole him from her or that I was making a play for him while they dated. I never did that. Anyway, over time we drifted apart and went on with our lives. We still spoke every now and then and sent Christmas cards over the years but our friendship never really recovered. I lost a very good friend because I was too afraid to be honest. One of the biggest regrets of my life."

I pat her on the shoulder. "I'm sure she knew that."

"I suppose," she replies. "I don't think she had any issue with Charles because she fell madly in love with your grandfather. Her issue was with me and my dishonesty."

I nod my head. "You know, before you came out here I was thinking about how I got to this point. I really feel like I was meant to find her journal, like it all happened for a reason."

She reaches for my hand. "I completely agree and that's why I was so happy to meet you. But then when you mentioned the journal, I was afraid of what it said about me. I wanted to tell you the truth but I was embarrassed . . . I wish I had explained everything to her and apologized."

I can see the regret in her eyes and I feel sorry for her. I can't imagine how it must feel to let all these years pass and never resolve a conflict.

"Who knows? Maybe my finding the journal and meeting you was her way of telling you that she forgives you." Her eyes fill with tears and she hugs me.

"Thank you." She whispers, "Or maybe we were supposed to meet because for some other reason, like . . ."

"Gran, what are you doing?" Trevor interrupts us. "Mom's in there ready to lose it because you aren't mingling."

I can see the annoyance on Beatrice's face as she rolls her eyes. I try to hide my smile.

"Are you blind? I'm mingling with one of my guests right here."

I stand back while Beatrice rants about spending the time at her birthday party the way she wants. It's kind of funny to see her acting like a child. She finally stomps off leaving me with Trevor. Neither of us says a word.

"So," he says. Oh my gosh, why the hell is this so awkward? "Sorry I interrupted your conversation."

"That's okay. I'm pretty used to it by now." I smile playfully. He catches my eye and for the first time I notice something different. Maybe it's my imagination but I suddenly feel a strange connection, or has it been here this whole time?

"Oh really, and what's that supposed to mean?" he says as he moves closer to me. All of a sudden, my heart starts to race but I don't move away. What the hell is wrong with me?

"Hmm . . . well, you seem to keep popping up wherever I am. I'm starting to wonder if you're doing it on purpose," I reply sarcastically. "Maybe you were the one who ran into me and made me spill my drink on you?"

I'm expecting some kind of smart-ass reply but what I get is shocking.

"Maybe I am doing it on purpose."

For the first time since I met Trevor, he seems to be serious, dead serious.

"You're funny," I say nervously as I punch him on the arm, expecting some kind of delayed joke.

He grabs my wrist as I punch him and pulls me closer to him. Our faces are now inches apart. This can't be happening, my sweet Kyle is right inside. I'm a horrible person.

"What are you doing?" I say as I pull away even though I really don't want to. I wait for him to say something.

"I don't know but I'm not going to pretend that I don't feel something." He moves closer to me again. "Let's be serious, we run into each other at a party and then meet again at my Gran's house. What are the chances?"

I turn away because I don't want to do this. I don't want to hurt Kyle and I don't want to make a mistake.

"This is crazy," I say loudly.

"I know," he whispers in my ear. "I'm sorry if I'm making you feel uncomfortable."

Uncomfortable does not even come close to how I'm feeling. I have so many emotions going on right now that I don't know what to do or say. I glance back through the French doors into the ballroom where I see Giselle. That's just the reminder I need that no matter what we are feeling out here, our lives are right inside those doors.

"Wait." I stop him as he leans in toward me. "Are you forgetting someone?" I point to Giselle. I'm sure she will go postal if she comes out and catches us caught up in this moment.

"No, I haven't forgotten," he says sadly. I knew it, as soon as I bring up Giselle his tone changes. It's understandable that we feel a connection but it's also possible that we both have gotten a little caught up in a strange situation.

I nod my head. "I thought so." We both stand there awkwardly again.

"I better get back in there. I've been gone way too long and I'm sure Kyle's looking for me." He doesn't stop me as I walk away, leaving him alone. I think it's about time for us to leave because as far as I'm concerned, this party is over.

# Chapter 14

I really wish someone would give me an answer. I think I've become completely desperate because as soon as I get home from the party I start looking up psychics online. I've never actually been to a psychic because I'm really scared of what they're going to tell me. But at this point, I don't know what else to do.

I couldn't wait to leave Beatrice's party. After the strange encounter with Trevor, I joined Kyle in the corner and didn't move from that spot. Cassie relentlessly asked me to talk to her in private again but I managed to avoid it. After Katherine's big cake presentation, we all gathered to say our good-byes to Beatrice and her family. Giselle was standing along with them as if she's a permanent member of their family. And maybe she is.

Trevor and I made eye contact a few times but I quickly looked away. Unfortunately, my very observant sister was watching the whole thing. As soon as I get home, I turn my phone off. I wouldn't be surprised to get a knock at my door in the middle of the night.

Kyle didn't really say much on the ride home. I'm a little paranoid that he saw something while I was outside with Trevor. Truthfully, things have been different since the New York trip, so much so that I'm starting to wonder if things will ever be the same again.

I finally give up on my psychic search and crawl into bed.

"Maris."

I open my eyes and look around. Okay, I admit I'm starting to freak out; maybe all of this stress is causing me to become a sleepwalker. Somehow, I ended up in the park around the corner from home, but I have no idea how I got here.

"Maris."

I look around to see who's calling my name. The voice is coming from behind the most beautiful lilac bushes I've ever seen. Just then she appears.

"Oh my gosh . . . Grandma?"

I can't believe this is happening. I run across the grass to her outstretched arms. I feel the warmth as her arms wrap around me.

"That was a beautiful performance, my darling," she says softly. Oh my gosh! It was her all along in those dreams. I can't believe I didn't recognize her voice before now, but it's definitely her because she calls everyone "darling."

"How are you here right now?" I ask. She looks at me

and caresses my cheek.

"What do you mean?" She laughs. "I've been here all along."

I think I'm going to cry because somehow deep down I knew it was her. I have so much I want to say to her that I don't know where to begin.

"Grandma, I found your journal and then everything got crazy. My life is such a mess right now and I don't know how to fix it. Please tell me what to do," I beg.

She stares at me with her sparkling blue eyes. I think I'm still in shock that she's here, wait until I tell Cassie. She totally gets into all of this stuff.

"You will make the right decision, you just need to follow your heart," she replies.
Ha, that's easier said than done. That wasn't the answer I was hoping for. I start to ramble on about the journal and Beatrice and New York. She just continues to smile at me, but she still doesn't give me any answers.

"I love you, my darling. Remember to follow your heart." She reaches up and places her hand on my cheek and then she turns around and starts walking back toward the lilac bushes.

That's it? She's leaving?

"Wait, where are you going?" I yell. All of a sudden, I'm standing alone in the middle of the park and she's gone.

"Wait," I yell again.

"Maris, wake up." I sit up, and all of a sudden, I'm back in my bedroom. Georgie is standing over me looking really pissed off.

"You were screaming."

"I'm sorry I woke you," I apologize and look around my room.

"I think you woke the whole city," she yells as she heads back to her room.

I look at the time and it's 4:30 a.m., that dream seemed so real. I lie back down and try to force myself to go back to sleep. I wish I could be back with my Grandma. Without thinking about it, I kick the covers off, put on my shoes, and head to the park.

Okay, I admit it may be a little insane to go to the park at this time of night or morning or whatever it is, but I have to do it. I walk-run around the corner and of course the park is empty. I sit down on my bench; I guess it was all a dream. I think back to what she told me, follow my heart. How am I supposed to do that when I don't know what's in my heart? I sit for a while and think about everything that's been happening. My relationship with Kyle was fine until I started thinking about moving. Am I just being selfish? I mean, Kyle just got the job he had been hoping for and I expect him to just pick up and leave? I know how hard he has worked. That's not fair of me to expect that of him.

Then there's Trevor—he's this handsome and mysterious stranger that I met on accident, then the shocker that he turns out to be Beatrice's grandson. Am I the only one who has been ignoring something that's been staring me in the face? I know I was meant to meet Beatrice, but what about Trevor? Was I really meant to meet him, too?

Before I think any more about my personal life, I have to make it through this recital. I have a few a few days and I still have a lot of work to do. My eyes start to feel heavy, so I start to head back to my apartment when something in the grass catches my eye. I walk over to see what it is and I get chills all over my body. It's a lilac! I look around the park for the trees that were in my dream, but there are none. I pick up the flower and smile— it wasn't just a dream after all.

This girl has become a complete nightmare. I'm sitting here in my rehearsal with Mimi and she's out of control. We have two more rehearsals left before the recital and I have considered quitting more times than I can count. A few days ago, Sophie even came in to give me a pep talk. Lucy has one more meeting planned for tomorrow and I'm dreading that as well. Somehow Ash and I have managed to completely avoid each other even when we had to run through the show.

"I think I'm done for the day," Mimi says as she picks up her books. We've been rehearsing for forty-five minutes but only have had about twenty minutes of quality rehearsing time. The rest of the time has been nothing but complaining and whining.
I really want to tell her to go ahead and leave but I ask her for one more run-through.

"I'm ready. I'll see ya tomorrow," she says as she picks up her Vera Bradley backpack and throws it over her shoulder.

I'm completely exhausted, which is not surprising considering my middle of the night rendezvous in the park. I slowly make my way to my closet-office to go over some notes and hopefully lay my head down on my desk for just a few minutes.

I'm just about to drift off when there's a knock on my door.

I groan. "I'm busy," I yell but they obviously don't take my hint.

"What is it?" I open the door ready to strangle the person on the other side.

I'm shocked to see Trevor standing there. What's he doing here?

"Hi, I'm sorry to bother you but I need to talk to you." He's practically begging, and honestly seeing Trevor beg is kind of funny (and hot!).

"Fine. Welcome to my closet-office." I hold my hand out to welcome him. He walks in and looks around and I see a tiny smile cross his face.

"What?" I fold my arms, giving him a dirty look.

"Nothing," he says, smiling. "Your office is cute."

I can't help but smile, too. "It sucks and you know it."

Somehow my little office inspires Trevor to tell me about the first apartment he lived in when he went to NYU. Of course, I remember that I learned he went to school in New York when I stalked him on social media. He claims his apartment was about the same size as my tiny space. I'm totally enthralled with his stories about living in New York that I start asking him a lot of questions.

"Why are you so interested in New York?" he asks. I guess I didn't hide my excitement very well, so I tell him all about my dream to perform on Broadway and about how I'm thinking about moving.

"You're thinking about moving to New York? When?"

I immediately regret saying anything.

"I don't know." I shrug. "I haven't figured everything out yet."

"Well, I'd be happy to give you some tips," he replies. "I know the city like the back of my hand. I always thought I'd make it back there someday."

Figures. Why does everything about Trevor appear to be so perfect? And now he's telling me that he would live in my favorite place in the world.

"Anyway," I say, changing the subject before I say or do something I regret. "What are you doing here?" We got so caught up in our conversation about New York that I don't even know why he randomly showed up at the studio.

He shifts from one foot to another. "Oh yeah, I wanted to talk to you about what happened at the party. I felt really bad about . . . well, everything. I shouldn't have put you in that position."

I can't believe he's apologizing. As bad as this makes me feel, I don't want him to apologize.

"I've thought about it non-stop and I'm sorry."

I'm not sure what has come over me but I want to know how he really feels.

"So, you're saying that you were wrong? That you don't feel anything?" I look him straight in the eye because I want to know the truth. I want to know if he has just been playfully flirting with me or if he does feel something more.

"No. I do feel something but maybe the timing's wrong or maybe . . ." he hesitates. "I mean, we're both in relationships and I don't want to be the cause of people getting hurt. Truthfully, things aren't good for Giselle and me, but that started long before I met you. I'm not sure we'll make it, but there's more to it than this." He points back and forth between us. "On the other hand, I've met Kyle and he's a decent guy."

Decent? Ha! Kyle is a saint.

"Although, as much as I like Kyle . . ." He stops and winks at me.

I really wish he wouldn't do that.

"So, you aren't as honorable as you are acting?" I ask coyly. I'm going to hell. Seriously, why can't I push this guy away? Maybe it really is fate or whatever they call it in the movies . . . Kismet? Is that what it's called? I need to Google that later.

Trevor moves closer to me, his face inches from my face. "No, I'm not."

Yep. I'm definitely going to hell. He kisses me softly and . . . wow . . . pretty much one of the most amazing kisses I've ever experienced.

I push him away, not because I want to but because it's the right thing to do. I have to talk to Kyle and find out where we stand.

"What? Why are you pushing me away?" he whispers. "Don't fight it."

Just then there's a knock. "Maris, you there?"

Shit! It's Sophie; I'm about to be caught with a man in my office who's not Kyle. I must have a look of horror on my face. "Tell her to go away," Trevor whispers.

Before I have time to panic, Sophie throws the door open. "Maris, we have to talk. Oh . . ." She looks at Trevor who's now leaning casually against the wall. He really has his innocent act down. That should probably throw up a red flag for me. I need to say something quick.

"I'm sorry for interrupting." Sophie can't seem to take her gaze off Trevor—not that I blame her.

"Not at all," Trevor says smoothly. "Trevor Ericson." He holds out his hand. "I just stopped by to get some information on the recital."

"I'm Sophie," she says sweetly. "I'm an instructor here as well. So, you're attending the show?"

"Yes, I want to bring my Gran; it's going to be a surprise." He looks at me.

I still haven't said anything. Nothing like awkward silence to make myself appear extremely guilty. I'm not as good at being a player as Trevor obviously is. And what is he talking about, bringing Beatrice to the recital?

"Sophie, Beatrice is Trevor's Gran. She was a good friend of my grandmother's. She just turned ninety, remember I told you about that birthday party I was attending?" I say, trying to sound as innocent as possible.

Now, I don't even remember if I told Sophie about the party. I may have mentioned a party but left out any details.

"Oh, sure," she says. Yeah, she's pretty much the worst liar ever. Trevor must sense that this awkwardness is not going away.

"Anyway, it sounds like you two have work to do. Thanks for the info, Maris. Gran is going to be ecstatic." He smiles confidently. "Pleasure meeting you, Sophie, hopefully I will see you again."

Sophie starts to blush and I roll my eyes.

"Thanks, Trevor. Have a good one." I practically push him out the door to face Sophie and her questions. Did I just say *Have a good one?* Lame.

"Is he single?" she asks immediately. I think about the miserable Giselle and her painted on gold dress from the party.

"Actually, he's not," I say nonchalantly. I'm not lying because he does have a girlfriend and he just kissed me, so I guess that makes him far from single. When I think about it, I feel horribly guilty and who knows, Trevor could possibly have a long list of women he flirts with especially if his relationship with Giselle hasn't been good for a while.

"Bummer," she says, disappointed.

"What did you need to talk to me about?" I ask, trying to change the subject.

She must be still thinking about Trevor because she looks at me like I'm speaking another language.

"Remember, you came in here saying you need to talk to me? Like five minutes ago?" I remind her.

"Oh, yeah," she exclaims. "I was walking by Lucy's office and Ash was in there. She was complaining about the order of performances and something else. Lucy's going to lose it on her, I know it."

Ha. If I had a dollar for every time I've thought that, I would be rich. I remind Sophie of the many times that we had thought Ash had pushed Lucy to the edge and nothing ever happened. So, I doubt it will happen now.

I hear my phone ringing from somewhere in my bag and see Kyle's calling me, so I kick Sophie out of my office, nicely of course.

A few minutes later, I hang up the phone and again I

feel like the worst person on the planet. Kyle invited me over for a home-cooked dinner the night after the recital, and of course I couldn't say no. He also said he had something very important to talk to me about. All of sudden I feel sick to my stomach because I know that this talk is long overdue for both of us.

# Chapter 15

There's nothing that compares to a good night's sleep. I've never been someone who has required a lot of sleep but lately I've been exhausted. I mostly blame the recital, which has quickly turned into the Ash show, but also the situation with Kyle and Trevor. Who would have thought that I would be in some weird love triangle saga? Although, I'm not really in an actual love triangle, but in my head it sure does feel like I am.

Today's the day of the big recital. Lucy is bringing us all in for another quick meeting. Well, hopefully it's quick because I have a million things to do.

Cassie called me to give me one of her little pep talks and for once I appreciated it. I will never actually admit that to her though.

It appears as though I will have quite the cheering section attending the show. My parents and Cassie have attended every recital or performance I've ever been a part of. It never mattered if my students were performing or I was performing, they've always come to support me. Of course, Kyle and Georgie will be there. I haven't talked to Beatrice, so I don't know if Trevor will actually be bringing her. He totally could have made that up to save me from Sophie. However, if they don't show that will definitely save me some stress and save me from listening to Cassie's advice on how I should live my life.

When I arrive at the studio, Lucy is in her office on a call. I'm making myself a plate of food when Ash walks in. We completely ignore each other until it occurs to me that I should suck it up and be the better person. I really hate having a conscience.

"Hey, I just wanted to say good luck tonight," I say convincingly. I do my best to make that sound like I mean it but I'm not sure how convincing I was. She stares at me in complete shock.

"Good luck to you, too," she replies finally.

We both stand there in silence. Oh well, at least I was the one to take the first step. I just wish someone was here to witness it. Thankfully, Lucy rushes in and starts the meeting. Truthfully, this meeting is completely unnecessary being that she wants to meet again before the show. I can tell I'm not the only one who's over her meetings. Even Ash who normally agrees to everything Lucy says doesn't look thrilled. I know Lucy's nervous and I get it because I'm nervous too, but we should be using this time to prepare.

A few hours later, I'm at the park doing some last-minute rehearsing in private. I'm performing a duet with Sophie as well as one of my own songs. I will also accompany two of my students for their performance.

I'm a little on edge about Mimi; she's been so unpredictable, so you never know what she may do. For all I know, she and Ash could have something crazy planned and once they're on stage there's nothing I can do about it. Georgie really wanted to come to the park with me but I begged her not to; I just wanted a few more minutes to collect my thoughts. I haven't been to the park since the night of my dream and maybe I've completely lost it, but a part of me is hoping that I will see Grandma again. I'm off in a daze when I look at the time and realize that I'm going to be late. I grab my bag and rush to my car. Tonight could change everything for me, and I'm hoping this may be exactly what I need to finally push me to make a decision. My nerves continue to build and I grip the steering wheel even tighter.

"Now don't forget how important this night is for our studio," Lucy reminds us for the hundredth time. "I need you all to be friendly and professional and that means putting aside all differences." She looks in my direction. That wasn't obvious or anything, she clearly thinks that I'm the cause of the issues with Ash. I want to defend myself and tell her that I was the one to wish Ash good luck this morning but it's really not worth it.

A text from Georgie takes my mind off Lucy and Ash.

This audience is getting crowded.

What does she mean by that? Is she trying to stress me out more than I already am? I text her back.

What is that supposed to mean?

I wait patiently for her to write back and of course she

doesn't. As soon as Lucy finishes her rambling, I head out to the audience to greet people. I spot Georgie across the room; she's standing with my family and Kyle. And then I see Cassie with Beatrice and Trevor. My heart sinks into my stomach. Of all the people that they have to talk to why does it have to be Cassie? I can only imagine what she's saying to him; she's probably giving him the third degree about his life.

I manage to grab Georgie so we can talk in private.

"Ow, why are you pinching me?" she cries.

"Are you going to tell me what you meant by your text?" I ask.

She gets a mischievous look on her face.

"Don't you think it's obvious? Your loyal boyfriend Kyle is here but so is the mysterious and charismatic Trevor. They're both here to see you . . . how does that make you feel?"

How does that make me feel? Where do I begin? I definitely don't have enough time to get into this right now.

"Hmm . . . well, Kyle is my boyfriend so I would expect him to be here and Trevor brought Beatrice tonight so that doesn't exactly mean he's here to see me. Does that answer your question?"

She gives me a look that clearly says "yeah, right."

"I have to greet more people before I check on my students, so just be a good best friend and wish me luck." She leans in to give me hug. We join the rest of my cheering section.

"There's my girl!" Kyle says excitedly. He wraps his arms around me. I can see Trevor squirming out of the corner of my eye. At least it looks like he's squirming, Beatrice raises her eyebrows at him and Cassie looks around smugly.

"Thank you all for coming tonight, it means so much. I have to go warm up with my students, but I will see you all after the show. We have an awesome after party planned and everyone is invited." I rush to head backstage in order to escape my family when I run into Miranda.

"Maris, there you are, I just spoke to Lucy. She can't stop talking about how fantastic this show will be. I'm looking forward to seeing all this new talent, and I hear that you will be performing an original song. I had no idea you wrote."

Here's my chance for some self-promotion. I may as well take advantage of it.

"Yes, I've been writing for years—but I just recently finished my first song. I have several that are in progress, but I'm performing this one for the first time tonight." As soon as I actually say that out loud I start to get extremely nervous. I don't usually get stage fright, but all of a sudden I feel like I could puke all over her.

"I better get backstage. I hope you enjoy the show." I run out before I humiliate myself.

False alarm! I rush to the bathroom, but luckily, I don't get sick. Everything seems to be right on schedule—the students are warmed up and anxious to get started. I even saw Mimi wishing everyone good luck and she looks happy. It's as if she's become a different person overnight.

We're beginning the show with a vocal ensemble featuring me, Sophie, Lucy, and Lilly. It was no surprise that Ash chose not to perform in this number. I can see Miranda sitting directly front and center; she looks as if she could be a member of the press with her notebook and iPad ready to record. Here we go . . . all our hard work is about to pay off. It's showtime!

# Chapter 16

It never ceases to amaze me how music can uplift and inspire people. I've been a part of many performances in my life, but tonight's show is simply magical. Every performance brings me to tears, laughter, and joy. The only time I feel a tinge of disappointment is when Mimi and Ash perform a duet. I admit I'm offended, but in the end, I'm really not surprised.

My solo goes perfectly. As I sing my last note, I look out into the audience at my family and friends. Kyle looks so proud and I just wish that I could fully share all of this with him, but something is missing. I see Beatrice and Trevor cheering just as loudly as anyone. I just hope no one reads more into that, and when I say no one, I mean Cassie and Georgie.

After the finale, I sit down in the dressing room and put my head down on the vanity. We did it and it was amazing. I have so many emotions going on right now—I'm happy, relieved, proud, and sad. The funniest thing is the first person that comes to my mind is Grandma; it's almost as if she is here with me.

"Maris, how amazing was that show?" Sophie comes in, interrupting my private moment. "Oh, and bravo on your solo, that song was a-mazing!"

Just then, the students join us, and I hear Lucy in the hall. "Everyone please join me in the dressing rooms."

Lucy comes in and immediately starts crying. "Well, family, we have another show under our belts. I can't begin to express how proud I am of each and every one of you. All the hours of rehearsing and dedication have truly paid off." Everyone starts to cheer.

"Now we have a fabulous after party planned, so please bring your family and friends to celebrate the tremendous talent we have here at Do-Re-Mi Studios." More cheers and whistles erupt and everyone starts talking at once.

I start to gather my things when Lucy comes over to me. "Maris, why have you not told me that you've been writing songs? All this time and you never said a word? This could be huge for us."

I smile. "Honestly, I just started writing for fun. I never thought I would finish a song, let alone perform it."

I won't dare tell her that I'm thinking of quitting the studio. Tonight is obviously not the night to deliver that kind of news.

"Well, you did and it was the perfect addition to the show, so thank you." She pulls me in for a tight hug. I guess if she was mad at me for the whole Ash situation she must be over it now.

When I'm finally able to join my family in the lobby, I'm greeted with cheers from everyone and tears from my mom.

"Honey, you sounded like an angel," she says between her blowing her nose in a Kleenex.

"Maris, the performance was mesmerizing!" Cassie says.

Kyle kisses me on the cheek and hands me a gorgeous bouquet of roses.

"Perfection," he says as he flashes me a loving smile.

I notice Beatrice and Trevor standing off to the side. I assume they are trying to stay out of the way until Beatrice waves me over.

She grabs both of my hands. "You sounded just like her, your grandmother. I know she would be so proud tonight." She gives me a hug and I fight the urge to cry.

"Maris, it was flawless." Trevor adds. "We brought these for you; Gran said we had to bring flowers and we thought these were perfect."

I stand in shock as he hands me a bouquet—a bouquet of lilacs. They look like the same lilacs that were in my dream and the same lilac that I found on the ground in the park. I'm completely speechless at first.

"Where did you get these?" I ask. Trevor and Beatrice look back and forth at each other.

"The florist, why?" he says curiously. I realize that

everyone is staring at me now. I need to hurry and think of something to say

"Oh, I . . . um, they're just really pretty. Thank you so much." I sound like a complete idiot, but really, what are the chances that they would bring the same flowers? It has to be another sign that Grandma was with me today. I've been thinking about her a lot and I'm sure she would have loved to be here. I'm starting to get emotional again.

"Okay, who's ready to go to a party?" I shout. That definitely takes some of the attention off my strange reaction to the flowers. I try to ignore Cassie's curious glances. I will have to explain my dream to her even though I already know what she's going to say. I lead the way to the celebration trying to shake the fact that those flowers have to be more than a coincidence.

I think the best part of being involved in any performance has to be the after party. They're always so much fun. Maybe it's all mental, like it's some sort of stress release. It has always amazed me at how different people act prior to the shows compared to after. Even Ash has been somewhat cordial to me— not exactly nice but cordial. Miranda has definitely fallen all over Mimi as we all expected she would. Both Ash and I take credit for her training, and I'm careful not to remind everyone that she's been training with me for years as opposed to months with Ash. It would serve her right for all the hell she has put me through over the last several weeks, but since I'm a better person than her, I won't say anything.

Trevor and Beatrice leave the party pretty early because she's tired. I thank them again for the flowers. I get the feeling that Trevor wanted to say something else but he didn't, so who knows, maybe it's just my imagination or, more appropriately, my paranoia.

"We need to have a talk," Cassie whispers as she comes up behind me. I completely agree with her but this is not the place.

"Later," I reply and walk away to talk to my other guests.

Kyle and I haven't had much of a chance to talk to each other with everyone interrupting us. It looks like we will have to wait for the impending dinner to have our big talk. I have to admit I'm not looking forward to that at all. He's being very attentive as usual, affectionate and patient as people come up to talk to me. I wish I knew what he wanted to talk to me about so I can emotionally prepare myself.

The party is winding down, but the best part of the night for me is when Miranda pulls me aside and asks me to call her. I try not to look overly excited, but I really just want to jump up on the table and start dancing. Granted, I don't know what she wants me to call her about and I probably shouldn't get too excited just yet. I mean, I would hope that it's something about how much she enjoyed my original song and she would love to represent me and she knows that she will be able to get me in a Broadway production. Yes, I have thought about hearing those words from her, or anyone really. A girl can dream, right?

I'm saying good-bye to my family when Lucy stops us.

"You should be so very proud of Maris," she says as

she puts her arm around my mom. "She has made me very proud, she's an integral part of this studio, and I know we have a beautiful future ahead of us."

Mom starts crying again and thanks her. I just hang back while they share this moment. I love Lucy and Do-Re-Mi Studios, but I can't help but think that it may be time for me to move on. I just have a feeling that there's more out there for my music career and me. I look over at Kyle who's talking to Georgie and Sophie. I don't know if he's ready to move on with me or not and that makes me sad, but I may not be the one that's enough for him either. He deserves someone who will be completely devoted to him also, and I don't know that I can be that way for him right now.

"I'm really looking forward to dinner tomorrow night," Kyle says when we finally have a few minutes alone with each other before he leaves.

"Me, too." I smile. "I'm sorry I haven't had a chance to spend much time with you tonight, you know how crazy these parties can be."

He nods. "Of course. You were fantastic tonight. It's completely expected that everyone would want a few minutes of your time. You really stole the show."

That's very nice of him to say, but I really don't think I stole the show. I think all of our students were fantastic with Mimi leading the way.

"Thank you, Kyle." When I give him a hug, I start to feel really emotional again. Maybe I'm PMSing? After he's gone, Georgie is my last remaining guest.

"Awesome show, girlfriend. I'm going to stop by the hospital on my way home. Dr. Scott is on call tonight, so I told him I'd grab some food with him."

I'm actually relieved that she won't be home right away because I'm exhausted and I know she would want to talk about everything that happened tonight. I can't wait to get home and crawl into bed. I have a feeling tomorrow is going to be another emotional day. I'm about to leave when Sophie stops me.

"We did it," she exclaims. "Do you think Miranda is going to pursue Mimi? Did you see Ash following her around? She was so obvious; I got the feeling Miranda wasn't that impressed with her. I'm sure Miranda has handled girls like Ash before."

I can tell that Sophie really wants to keep talking, but I'm just so tired. I tell her that I will call her tomorrow so we can talk more.

"Wait!" She puts her hands on my shoulders. "I have to ask you one more thing, are you sure that Trevor has a girlfriend?" she asks curiously. I hope she doesn't ask me to try to set her up with him. I'm not the best matchmaker, especially for a man I have a (small) crush on.

"Yes. Why?"

She gets a mischievous look on her face. "I'll tell you why, because he watched you the entire night. I think he likes you." Okay, I didn't expect her to say that. "That's ridiculous, we're just family friends." This is true, we are family friends . . . sort of.

"I knew you would say that, but trust me when I tell you that I'm really good at sensing this kind of stuff. My aunt had the sixth sense and they say it's hereditary."

Holy crap, Sophie thinks she's a medium. Here I was searching the Internet for psychics and I've known one all along.

"Yeah, I don't think so. Anyway, I'm really exhausted, so can we talk tomorrow?" I have to get home or I may fall asleep at the wheel. I'm so glad this night is over, especially now.

# Chapter 17

Why won't people let me sleep? I finally turned off my phone after all the early morning phone calls. I don't know why I didn't do it last night. I was so tired that I barely made it to my bed. My mom has called three times to tell me that moving is officially taking place next week. Apparently, she wants the whole family to be at the new condo the first night. I've been ignoring this move but not entirely on purpose being that I've had plenty of my own drama to deal with. She says they're mostly packed up and ready, and according to Cassie, the new condo is very tranquil and Zen, whatever the hell that means.

Speaking of Cassie, she also called me this morning and I know exactly what she wants to talk about. I admit, I want to talk to her too but not when I'm trying to sleep. Thankfully, Georgie has left me alone but who knows what time she got in last night or if she's even home.

As I've been in and out of sleep, I'm trying to think about what I need to say to Kyle at dinner. I'm going to be honest with him and tell him that I have to give

NYC a try, if I don't I will always wonder. I can't go through my life like that and I wouldn't want to hold him back either. I have no doubt that I love him, but I'm still not sure that's enough.

When I finally realize that I'm not going back to sleep, I call Cassie back. I tell her all about my dream and seeing the lilac in the park.

"I'm so jealous," she exclaims. "Do you know how special it is for Grandma to visit you from the other side?" I knew she would believe me because this is totally her thing.

"So, you don't think it was just some stress-induced wild dream? It really happened?" I ask her. I'm relieved that I'm not completely losing my mind.

"No!" she says adamantly.

She goes on to ask me about Trevor. This was the part I was not looking forward to talking about but I know I have to. I fully unload on her—everything about Kyle and New York and the few moments I've had with Trevor.

"Wow," she says finally. "I think that's what Grandma meant by following your heart. You will have to decide if Kyle is what you want, but I think there may really be something there with Trevor, or maybe you are just meant to follow your heart to New York? Maybe she wasn't talking about anything having to do with your relationship or a man?"

Ugh! She's supposed to be helping me not confusing me even more. I thank her and tell her I will keep her posted on how things go at dinner tonight. One way or another, a decision has to be made.

~*~*~

"I'm so glad we can finally spend some time together." Kyle warmly welcomes me in when I arrive for dinner. He has a nice glass of wine waiting for me along with some delicious bruschetta for an appetizer. Did I mention that Kyle is an amazing cook? This is not a surprise considering he's almost the perfect man. I can only cook eggs, and that's on a good day. I probably won't make the best wife, but I can bake so I guess that's a plus. Georgie keeps asking me to take a cooking class with her. It's actually not a bad idea, but I would be afraid I'd burn the place down.

"Me, too." I smile. "I'm sorry again about last night; I hope it didn't seem like I was ignoring you."

"No, not at all. It was a busy and exciting night for you."

As soon as we are comfortably sitting down to dinner, Kyle starts to ask about my parents' move. "You haven't mentioned anything about it, but they told me last night that it's happening pretty soon." He gives me a sympathetic look.

"Yep. It's really happening," I tell him. "Mom wants me to come to the new place that night so that we can all be there together." I roll my eyes. "It really doesn't make any sense since they won't even be settled in yet. Unless she thinks we're all going to help them unpack?" Now I'm starting to wonder if that's why she wants us all there so badly.

Our conversation continues but I can see that Kyle is becoming a little more anxious. He keeps drinking his wine and pouring more. Before he gets drunk, he finally brings up the elephant in the room. "I invited you over because I wanted to talk. I know things didn't go the way you wanted them to in New York and that was my fault. I was so preoccupied with the promotion that I didn't consider you and your feelings at all."

"It's okay." I smile. "It was a work trip and I knew that when you invited me. I shouldn't have acted like a spoiled brat."

He grabs my hand. "Anyway, I know you said that you needed to think about things and make some decisions, so hopefully this will help." I really need to speak up as well, but it appears that he has this all planned out.

"I wanted to wait until after dinner to talk about this, but I've been so anxious and nervous about it. We've been together for too long for me not to show you how fully committed I am too you." I try to interrupt him but he stops and reaches in his pocket. He pulls out a small blue box and not just any blue box. The *Tiffany blue box* wrapped in the perfect white ribbon.

Wait. He's not. He can't be . . .

"Maris Forrester, I love you and I want to be with you . . . forever. I've been thinking about this for a while and the New York trip just made me realize that I needed to take this step."

This can't be happening. He is.

He gets down on one knee and opens the Tiffany blue

box and there it is. It has to be one of the most amazing rings I've ever seen. I don't take my eyes off of it until I hear the words, "Maris, will you marry me?"

I look up at his handsome face, his eyes are sparkling and his perfect white teeth are sparkling under his gorgeous smile. I feel like I'm dreaming again. I can't give him an answer yet, and I'm afraid I'm about to shatter his heart into a million pieces.

"Kyle." I grab his hand and motion for him to get up from the floor. "We need to talk." His sweet smile fades. "I love you, too, but this is moving really fast. Seriously, don't you think that we should talk about it before taking such an important step?" I explain my feelings to him and he listens without saying a word. I tell him that I think I should give New York a try and I know he has no desire to move there, especially with the new job. He shrugs his shoulders.

"I would never expect you to leave this opportunity that you've worked so hard for."

He still doesn't say anything as he stares out the window, so I continue talking.

"I told you when we were in New York that I would consider everything before making any decisions. Last night when I was on stage—I loved every second of it. It's the first place that I've felt like I belonged in a while . . . does that make sense?"

Silence.

"Kyle, please say something," I beg. I just hope he doesn't start crying. I keep eyeing the shiny thing that just came out of the Tiffany blue box. Wait until Georgie hears about this.

"So, let's just say that I would consider going to New York with you, would you accept my marriage proposal?" he asks finally. "You say you love me, but you seem so willing to just leave, like it's easy for you."

Wow. I have no idea how to answer that.

"It's not easy at all," I reply finally. "And even if you came to New York, which I would love, I still don't know if I'm ready to get married." I can see the disappointment on his face and I feel so guilty. I look around at the dinner he's prepared—complete with the wine, candles, music, and of course the blue box. Am I crazy? Most women only dream about the perfect man and the perfect proposal. I have both and I'm thinking of turning it down.

"Will you just take a few days to think about it?" he asks. Hmm . . . this is totally my chance to ask the same of him.

"I will, if you think about coming with me." I know that he won't come to New York, but it never hurts to ask.

"Okay," he agrees.

He asks me to hold on to the little blue box to which I decline. I don't need that gorgeous thing clouding my judgment.

He looks completely heartbroken. Okay, so maybe it's not that big of a deal for me to hold on to it, but it will stay in the box and not on my finger.

"Will you tell me one thing, though?" he asks. I nod my head.

"Do you like the ring?"

Is he crazy? Of course, I like it.

"Yes!" I exclaim. "I love it. I just don't want us to rush into something that we may regret later."

We don't say much while we clean up the dinner dishes. I know Kyle's upset and I know I completely ruined the evening. On my way home, I make a stop at the park to think and sing. I wonder if Kyle would consider moving with me now. Maybe he loves me enough to be patient as I follow a crazy childhood dream, but what about his dream and what he has been working for? Can I let him leave all of that behind?

As I'm getting ready for bed, I check my phone. As if my life isn't complicated enough. There's a text from Trevor.

Got your number from Gran. We should talk.

*I just need to follow my heart.* I remind myself. I just wish I knew which way it was taking me.

~*~*~

I walk in the door at my parents' house and look around at the bare walls and empty rooms and then I look longingly at the hardwood floor. I get a running start and slide along the floor toward the kitchen. I

# See You Soon Broadway

smile to myself, but I feel like crying. Why does everything have to change?

"Mom? Dad? Cassie?" I call.

"I'm so happy you're here, honey." Mom gives me a hug after I slide into the kitchen. I sit down at the kitchen table, which is still in the middle of the room. Cassie and Mom are wiping out the cabinets and wrapping items in newspaper. I guess Cassie has been helping Mom a lot. I'm such a brat. Other than going through my own boxes, I haven't lifted a finger to help. None of them have said a word about it, but I do feel a bit guilty.

Although, it seems like guilty is all I've been feeling lately. I haven't spoken to Kyle for a few days other than some texts back and forth. I'm still so confused, and I haven't told anyone about the proposal yet. I have the perfect little blue box in my bag, so I'm hoping I can get Cassie alone to show her. In the meantime, I finally responded to Trevor and told him I would be in touch soon. I reread the text over and over again. It sounded so terribly formal. My life is officially in shambles.

"Um, Cassie, when you have a minute I have a yoga question for you?" She stops what she's doing and gives me a curious look. She knows me well enough to know that there is no yoga question nor would there ever be a yoga question.

"Let's take a walk," she says eagerly. Mom is as oblivious as always and starts humming an Air Supply tune as she works. I know Air Supply tunes well since my parents have been obsessed fans for as long as I

173

can remember.

Cassie and I start to walk along the sidewalk. We're both quiet, but since I called this little meeting, I start talking first. "So, you know there isn't a yoga question but I wanted to show you something. I reach into my bag, pull out the perfect little blue box, and hand it to her. Her eyes get huge and she frantically opens it.

"Is this what I think it is?" she's practically screaming.

I nod my head slowly. "Yep, that would be an engagement ring from Tiffany's. Kyle proposed and I told him I would think about it and I started to . . ." I trail off and pull out my phone. "And then I got this." I show her the text from Trevor.

For the first time in my life, I think Cassie is as confused as I am. She keeps looking back and forth between the ring and the phone.

"Maris, are you in love with Kyle?" she asks. What kind of a question is that? Of course, I am. I think she senses my confusion, so she continues while rolling her eyes, "I know you love him, but are you in love?"

I think for a minute. "Yes. I think I am." I look down the street that I grew up on. I'm not going to get upset that this street will soon be only a memory.

"Maris?" she says, interrupting my thought.

"Cassie, is it possible to be in love but feel like something is missing?"

She nods her head. "Of course. Does this have

anything to do with Trevor?" Ha! Now that is definitely a harder question.

"I'm attracted to him," I reply, feeling uncomfortable admitting it out loud. "And I think he's extremely irritating and arrogant. He's so full of himself, but then at same time he has such a caring way about him, especially when it comes to Beatrice and that's very endearing." I look down at the ground.

"Well, little sister, as I've said before, only you can make this decision—but I will tell you that there are no such things as coincidences, and I truly believe that everything happens for a reason." It doesn't take a genius to understand what she's trying to say. I know I need to talk to Trevor.

When we get back from our walk, I grab my phone and go into my parents' room. It's the only room in the house that seems to still be intact. I lie down on my parents' bed and nervously dial Trevor's number. Our conversation goes really well and we plan to meet at Starbucks the next day because that's always the best place to meet. Also, in my head, it seems completely safe and innocent to meet him for coffee.

"Well?" Cassie whispers when I join them downstairs. I tell her about our big plans to meet for coffee. She gives me the look of approval and all of a sudden she has plenty of advice to give.

"You know you will feel much better when you guys finally have this conversation but, before you jump into anything, find out what Kyle has decided. You need to give him every chance possible."

"What does Kyle have to decide?" Mom asks, interrupting our whispering. I guess we weren't being as quiet as I thought we were. I really don't want to get into this with my mother.

Thankfully, Cassie saves the day. "Just job stuff, Mom." She's always been so good at quick responses.

When I get home, I decide to straighten up my room. Ever since I decided to finish my song and perform it, I've let everything else go. My room could possibly be condemned at any moment. I start to move around the mess, starting with organizing my songbooks. Underneath the pile of junk, I find Grandma's journal. I look through the pages to see where I left off. She never finished writing in it and most pages have just one or two lines written on them. I flip toward the end of the journal and after several blank pages I find one last entry.

*I've learned a lot over the course of this amazing career and I'm so incredibly happy to be able to do what I love. I've met an amazing man and I see a wonderful future ahead for us. I have learned that true joy will come if you . . . follow your heart.*

Oh wow. That's the same thing she told me. I know she's talking about my grandpa in this entry. I'm going to listen to her advice and follow my heart, but I also know that someone will be hurt in this process. I pull the perfect little blue box out of my bag and open it. For the first time, I take the ring out and slip it on my finger. It's absolutely stunning.

"Holy crap, is that a ring?" Georgie yells. I jump

straight up in the air. I was so focused on what I was doing that I didn't hear her come home. I'm about to explain, but she doesn't let me get a word in. "I had a feeling this was coming. Kyle would never want to lose you and now you can stay here. I would've been devastated if you moved."

I don't know what to say. I sit on the bed and stare at the beautiful ring on my finger. I know I would be happy with Kyle, so maybe marrying him isn't the wrong decision. I take the ring off and put it back in its perfect little box.

"Maris, why are you taking your engagement ring off?" she asks with a horrified look on her face.

"Because I'm not engaged," I say flatly. I watch her expression change as she's processing what I just told her. "I didn't accept Kyle's proposal . . . yet." I hold up my hand. "Before you say anything, let me explain."

Georgie, being the good friend she is, listens patiently even though I can tell she wants to interject several times, but she lets me finish.

"Okay, so let me get this straight, you will have coffee with Trevor tomorrow and depending on how that goes then you will give Kyle an answer to his marriage proposal?" She falls back on my bed dramatically (as usual). "I feel like we're in a movie or a soap opera," she exclaims.

I fall back onto the bed next to her. I can't disagree with her. What seemed like an easy decision has become incredibly difficult, and now I'm so paranoid that I will make the wrong decision. There's still the fact that the power-couple consisting of Trevor and Giselle will stay together, so he may not even be available. I could be completely jumping to the wrong conclusion, maybe he wants to talk about Beatrice or maybe he has decided to finally give me the dry-cleaning bill for his suit. Here I am telling Georgie that I may have to choose between two men and one technically isn't even available. Now I know that I've completely lost it.

"Kyle actually said he would consider coming to New York," I say. "As in he would actually consider leaving his life and his new job behind to be with me." Wow. When I say it out loud I'm amazed . . . how stupid am I to even consider letting a guy like that slip away?

"Kyle is a great guy—there's no doubt about that," Georgie replies. I'm glad she's oblivious to what I'm really thinking because she would probably try to convince me to stay and marry him, and this *has* to be my decision.

"Yeah, he's the best." I agree.

# Chapter 18

I'm completely shocked to get a call from Liv being that I haven't spoken to her since the impromptu girls' dinner. I'm even more shocked to hear that Miranda couldn't stop talking about the recital and my song. What? I've been so consumed with all my relationship and non-relationship drama that I completely forgot about Miranda asking me to call her. I will have to do that later because right now I'm too busy being a nervous wreck as I get ready to meet Trevor for coffee. Seriously, I'm so nervous that you would think I was going on a job interview. I keep glancing at the little blue box that's still sitting on my nightstand. I admit that I've put the ring on my hand two more times since Georgie caught me with it, and the marriage proposal doesn't seem so scary anymore.

Trevor is already there when I arrive at Starbucks. I can see him through the window. He's sitting there dressed in another obviously expensive suit reading *Forbes Magazine*. Typical.

He smiles when he sees me and stands up when I get

to the table. "Thanks for meeting me today," he says. He even pulls out the chair for me. Who still does that? No doubt that would be the influence from his mother and grandmother.

"Sure," I reply nervously.

There's a weird awkward moment between us until we start talking at the same time.

"I just thought we should talk," he says at the same time I say, "So, you wanted to talk." We both laugh nervously.

"Go ahead," I tell him. I want to hear him out before I say anything stupid.

"Well, to start, Giselle and I had a huge fight the other night and we broke up." Okay, that's a positive start to our conversation. I try not to look happy even though I'm dying to jump up and cheer. "Like I told you before, things haven't been good between us for a while. It has felt like I've been on a rollercoaster and I'm tired of trying to make something work that isn't." I can tell that he's being completely honest, so I listen intently. "Don't get me wrong, things between us physically have always been fantastic but emotionally we aren't there." I clench my fists under the table and may or may not throw up in my mouth a little. Now I wish I wasn't listening so intently. Really, he could have left that part out but I try not to show my disgust.

"Anyway, I have a confession to make," he says. I take a deep breath because you never know what's going to be revealed when someone says that.

"The night at Liv and Tom's party, Giselle and I had another big fight. I spent most of the night trying to make up with her but she wasn't having it. So, I finally sat down in the corner, just drinking and feeling sorry for myself until I saw you wandering around. Something about you . . . I don't know, I guess I felt drawn to you."

He stares into my eyes and I feel my heart speed up. My mind starts screaming at me, this is wrong and I think about the little blue box sitting at home on my nightstand.

"So, you're saying that you ran into me that night?" I reply sarcastically.

He cracks a smile. "I did—well, not on purpose." He adds, "I was just going over to talk to you when you turned around and that's how you ruined my favorite suit." He winks at me.

I scowl. "Would you like me to buy you a new suit?" Of course, I have no intention of buying him a new suit, but honesty I'm getting tired of hearing about it.

"No—but I'm sure I can think of another way for you to pay me back," he replies with a wicked smile. I'm feeling so uncomfortable that I just blurt out the first thing that comes to my mind.

"Kyle proposed to me." I don't even know why that came out and now I'm even more uncomfortable. Trevor looks shocked.

"Excuse me, did you say he proposed to you?" he repeats calmly. "What did you say?" He's practically on the edge of his seat.

I inhale deeply. "I told him that I would think about it and I have been thinking about it."

"And?"

"And . . . there are a lot of factors to think about before I make such a huge decision." I want to say more but for some reason I hold back.

Trevor reaches over, grabs my hand, and looks into my eyes. All of a sudden, I feel like a silly teenager. My heart is beating faster and my mouth is dry.

"You can't marry him." I wait for him to say something else but he doesn't.

"Why?" I ask, returning his deep stare.

"Remember that day that I was at your studio?" he replies. "You were so excited about the prospect of moving to New York and following your dream. Kyle will only hold you back, you need to go to New York." He takes a sip of his coffee. That's it? That's the *only* reason he thinks I shouldn't marry Kyle.

"I haven't given up on that," I say, pulling my hand away. "Kyle even said he would consider coming with me." All of a sudden, I feel confused. Trevor invited me here to tell me that he and Giselle broke up, but he hasn't said anything else other than that I should move to New York. I'm growing more and more agitated.

"Can I ask you why you wanted to meet today?" I ask.

"I told you, I wanted to make a confession about the night we met and to tell you about Giselle and I breaking up." He starts to fidget, which seems so strange considering how put together he appears to be. "Maris, I don't want to complicate things further for you. There's no doubt that I feel a connection to you, but at the same time, just getting out of a relationship, I don't know that I'm ready to jump right into something serious."

I don't believe this—I feel like such a fool. I'm about to tell him where he can shove his mixed signals but I don't want to let on that I was expecting more.

"You're absolutely right," I say firmly. "I do need to go to New York, but I don't need your advice about my relationship. I can do what I want and *marry* who I want." I grab my bag and start to get up from the table.

"Wait, why are you upset?" he asks, grabbing my arm to stop me. "I was just trying to be honest. I would like to explore our attraction, but I can't commit to anything serious—at least not right now. Maybe we could just get to know each other better and you know . . . have fun."

I'm such an idiot. I was actually considering giving up a guy like Kyle for someone who just wants to *have fun*. Not that there's anything wrong with that, but Kyle is loyal and I know he loves me. Even if I decide not to marry him, New York should be the reason for that, not a fling with Trevor.

I sit back down so I don't make a scene in the middle of Starbucks. "Tell me, Trevor, how do you expect us to *get to know each other* when you just told me that I should move to New York?"

He starts to look as uncomfortable as I feel. "I don't know, I guess I could come visit you and I'm sure you will be back here to see your family."

I laugh sarcastically and shake my head. "Really, Trevor, I know what you meant by us having fun and no thanks." This time I leave despite his pleading and I don't look back.

I'm so pissed that I can't see straight. What the hell just happened? I can understand what Trevor meant about just getting out of a relationship and not wanting to be serious, but I guess I was expecting more. I pull off the highway and into the first parking lot I see. I have to figure out what to do with this mess I call my life. I find my phone and call Kyle. We agree to meet for dinner. It's time to finally decide what path my life needs to take. It's time to follow my heart.

# Chapter 19

"Maris, it's so great to hear from to you," Miranda says happily. As soon as I get home from my disastrous meeting with Trevor, I call Miranda. I want to have every bit of information I need before I see Kyle tonight.

"I'm so sorry for not calling sooner. Things have been, um, hectic since the recital." There really isn't a better word to describe the events that have gone down since that night. I guess I could say my life has been a nightmare, but I don't want her to think I'm a complete drama queen.

"That's quite alright," she says quickly. "Okay, I will just put this out there. I'm not sure what Livie told you, but I have an idea—well, more like an offer. We have a good friend who has a performing arts school here; she needs someone like you on her team. Would you ever consider a transfer?"

I feel as if I'm dreaming, so I smack myself a few times. I know it's basically a lateral move—I would go from one studio teaching to teaching at another—but it gets me to New York and I can't pass up any opportunities.

"You mean a transfer to New York?" I ask just to make sure I'm not hallucinating. "Yes, I would definitely consider it," I reply calmly despite my jumping up and down and running in circles in my room. I ask her for some details about the school so I can do some research, and she offers to give me a day or two to think about everything.

When I get off the phone I feel like I'm finally taking a step forward. I have a few more hours before I see Kyle, so I do the only thing I can think of—I go to the park and I bring the ring with me. After I belt out a few songs, I sit on my bench and I think. I think about my family, Grandma, Georgie, Beatrice, Trevor, and of course Kyle. I'm going to follow my heart the only way I can right now. I don't know if it's right or wrong, but I have to take a step forward.

~*~*~

"It's nice to see you," Kyle says as soon as we sit down at the table. So far so good—things don't seem weird, at least not yet.

"When's the big move?" he asks. At first I think he's taking about New York, but then I realize he's talking about my parents.

"Day after tomorrow," I say softly. "I think I'm finally okay with it though. I mean, I'm an adult and have to live my own life. I guess it was kind of silly of me to be so upset about it in the first place."

"No way." He disagrees. "The news took you by surprise. That's totally understandable."

We can't keep talking about my parents' move all night. One of us has to cut to the chase. Kyle must read my mind because he's the first to bring up the subject at hand.

"Maris, I thought about everything you said the other night." I bite my lower lip and take a deep breath while he continues. "I guess I didn't realize how serious you were about going to New York, and after watching you sing I can understand why. You were unbelievable and I think it's a great idea."

Oh my gosh. He finally gets it.

"Really?" I ask excitedly and I reach across the table to hold his hand. "Does that mean that you would come with me?"

His face falls and I already know what's coming before he says a word.

"Nothing would have made me happier than if you accepted my marriage proposal. But you didn't and you still aren't wearing the ring." He points at my left hand. "You don't want to get married, do you?"

I look down and shake my head slowly. "Not right now." A tear rolls down my cheek. "I'm sorry, Kyle. I have to go, if I don't I would always wonder. I would hate for that to happen and have it affect us." I take the perfect little blue box out of my bag and slide it along the table back to him.

He moves to my side of the booth and sits next to me wrapping his arms around me.

"Go!" he whispers in my ear. "If things are meant to be, it will work out." I sob on his shoulder leaving a huge wet stain. We sit for a while quietly; the server can obviously see that we're in the middle of something important so she leaves us alone. It was probably a bad idea to meet in public for this talk but it's too late now. I might be making the biggest mistake of my life, but as Kyle said, if it's meant to be, it will work out.

I'm a complete mess when I get home. After I calmed down, Kyle admitted that he didn't feel like moving was the right decision for him because he would have to start over in his own career. We agreed that we should take a break for us both to figure out what we really want. So, we are officially on a break (as in Ross and Rachel from *Friends*). I think we both know that New York will probably be a permanent move for me and there's no reason in prolonging the inevitable. He will never want to join me and I will probably never want to leave.

I fall into Georgie's arms as soon as I walk in.

"Oh no, honey!" she exclaims. "What happened? You look awful."

I can always count on Georgie for her honesty. No wonder everyone at the restaurant wouldn't stop staring at me. I'm definitely too afraid to look in the mirror.

She listens and rubs my back as I tell her about my day, starting with the coffee date from hell with stupid

Trevor and then the breakup with Kyle. As I repeat the events of the day, I can't help but feel sorry for myself. I started the day thinking I was in some complicated only-in-my-mind love triangle and I end the day completely alone. Not only that, but both men told me I should move. I'm sure that would be considered the ultimate rejection. I could probably go on a talk show with this story.

"There's something else I have to tell you," I say as I prepare to tell her that I am indeed moving. "There was one good thing that happened today, at least I think it's a good thing." I go on to tell her about Miranda's job offer and that I've decided to take it.

"I'm sorry, Georgie, I promise I will pay to break the lease or help you find a new roommate." I don't want her to think that I would ever leave her high and dry. Her response completely surprises me, and I'm once again reminded that she's the best friend anyone could ever have.

"What are you apologizing for? That's awesome news," she exclaims. "You made the right decision—I would even consider going with you if things weren't going *so* good with Dr. Scott, but they are." She stops and cringes. "Sorry, it's not really cool of me to talk about my relationship after the day you had."

Before I get a chance to tell her I'm happy for her, she starts in with Trevor. Not that I'm surprised.

"I just don't understand what happened with Trevor? He broke up with that horrible tramp then asks you to meet him only to tell you that he thinks you should leave town. What kind of jerk does that?" She makes it sound a little worse than it is. Maybe I overreacted?

"That basically sums it up, but don't forget that he wants to get to know each other and *have fun*." I use my fingers to make quotation marks. "I mean, I can understand him not wanting to jump into something else so quickly, but I guess I just feel stupid."

She nods her head. "Maybe, but you shouldn't feel stupid. He did lead you on."

Did he really lead me on? He had a girlfriend and I had a boyfriend—maybe we just got caught up in a strange situation. I think about our chance meeting at the event and again at Beatrice's combined with our mutual attraction. Still, I can't really blame him for not wanting to rush into a new relationship even though I'm kind of humiliated at his rejection.

"We both just got caught up in the whole thing." I try to blow it off because it really doesn't matter. It's time for me to start focusing on the future, starting with a call to Miranda first thing in the morning. I can't believe it's finally happening—I'm going to New York. Now, why am I not happy?

When I wake up the next morning, my eyes are all swollen and I'm all stuffy. I look in the mirror and quickly decide that I can't leave the house today and possibly tomorrow, which would get me out going to family fun night at the stupid new condo.

I start to feel a tiny bit better after I talk to Miranda. She's setting up a time for me to come check out the studio and meet Selena, the owner. She's being so helpful that I even go as far as to ask her to let me know if she hears of any places to live. There's so much to think about that it's somewhat overwhelming. I'm still not as excited as I expected I would be. Maybe it just hasn't sunk in yet that I'm really going to make the move. With all the anticipation and the back and forth trying to make a decision, when I finally do make a decision it feels like a letdown. What's wrong with me? And I refuse to blame it on being rejected by both Kyle and Trevor—I can't let these men take away the joy of finally doing something I've always wanted to do.

I sit down at the table and start to make a list of everything I have to do then it occurs to me that I will have to break the news to Lucy. I do feel a little sad at the thought of leaving Do-Re-Mi Studios and my students. I have many great memories there and I know I can thank Lucy for the opportunity sitting in front of me. At least I know that Ash will be thrilled with my news. Admittedly, it does give me satisfaction to know that Miranda offered this position to me and not her. A smile spreads across my face at that thought, and all of a sudden, I'm starting to feel better.

# Chapter 20

I finally leave my apartment to make the forty-five-minute drive to my parents' new home. When I walk in, I admit to myself that the condo is really nice even though I pretend to not be impressed. Cassie's right, too, it is kind of Zen—I'm still not exactly sure what that means, but it's very laid-back and beachy, so maybe that's what she meant by that. Mom gives me the grand tour as soon as I arrive. I can see how excited she is and I can't help but feel bad for all the grief I've given them.

"Follow me this way," she calls excitedly. "This room will be all yours when you come to stay." She takes me into a cozy little room with a gorgeous view, complete with a keyboard so I will be able to play my music. Ugh, now I feel even worse. I don't tell her that I will definitely need a place to stay now that I'm moving. I'm planning on giving them the news tonight when the whole family is together.

"Thanks, Mom, it's really nice." I wrap my arm around her shoulder. She gives me a look of satisfaction. I suppose she was hoping that this cute room would win me over and maybe it has, a little.

"Why didn't you bring Kyle tonight?" she asks. Ah . . . the dreaded question of the night. I'm about to break the news but Cassie and her mind reading powers interrupt us at just the right time.

"There you are," she says

I give her a grateful smile even though she has no idea that she saved me . . . or maybe she does.

"What do you think of the place?" Cassie asks me. Mom looks just as eager to hear my answer.

"It's really nice," I say sincerely. "I'm really happy for you, Mom." And this time I think I mean it.

After dinner, we're getting ready to play Sequence, my parents' favorite game. I know it's time for me to give the news.

"Hey, everyone, I have to tell you something," I announce. Silence comes over the room and Mom gives me a look of sheer terror.

"Oh no, Maris, did you go and get yourself pregnant? What are you going to do? Is that why Kyle isn't here tonight?" She keeps rambling without giving me a chance to stay another word.

"Mom, let her talk," Cassie says calmly. She looks at me curiously.

I plaster a big smile on my face as I explain the offer

that Miranda has given me and about my moving plans. My family seems surprised at first but then really happy for me. I don't have the heart to break the news regarding Kyle, but I know that I have to.

"There's one more thing." I interrupt the conversation and cheers. "Unfortunately, Kyle will not be coming with me, as you know he was recently given a huge promotion—we've decided to take a break while I see how things go with the new job." As I expected, this news didn't go over well. I knew my parents liked Kyle, but I had no idea that they would think I would give up a great career opportunity for a man.

"Are you sure this is the right move?" Mom asks worriedly. My dad who hardly ever speaks up starts to Google recent crime in New York City.

"I'm worried that you won't be safe on your own." He adds, "It would be better if Kyle was there."

I look longingly at Cassie for her help with trying to talk them off the ledge. She shrugs her shoulders at me. What? I can't believe she's not going to step in and help. I give her a dirty look. Is this punishment for my reaction to selling their house?

"I'm going to be fine," I reply. "I would've thought you would've been supportive of me. You know I've wanted this since I was a kid." I remind them of how I used to go to the library and look up New York City in the encyclopedia and on that microfiche thing. Those were the olden days before the Internet of course. I also remind them how I loved to watch any and all TV programs that were held at Radio City Music Hall and I've always been obsessed with the

Macy's Thanksgiving Day Parade and Dick Clark's New Year's Rockin' Eve. You would've thought I was talking to strangers by their responses. Finally, Cassie steps in to back me up—I'm convinced she was purposely trying to make me squirm for a little while.

"Finally," I whisper to her after my parents calm down. "Seriously, you couldn't have backed me up sooner?"

She opens her mouth to protest but then closes it. I roll my eyes.

"Wait, what happened with Trevor?" she whispers.

I scowl. "He's an ass." Then I walk to the kitchen to fill my wine glass. I never drink this much but in light of recent events in my life I guess I'm entitled to a few *extra* glasses of wine. Of course, Cassie is not satisfied by my answer and follows me to kitchen.

"What happened?"

I take sip and lean against the counter. "Well, let me see . . . he asked me to meet him for coffee. He told me he and that horrible girl broke up, then told me he thought I should move to New York." I pause to hear what Cassie has to say.

She looks perplexed. "What else?"

I smirk. "He felt a connection with me but doesn't want to get into anything serious. Oh . . . and maybe we can get to know each other and *have fun.*"

"Oh," she says, looking taken aback.

I place my now empty glass down on the counter. (*Wow, that went fast.*) "You know, the other night after our meeting I felt like such an idiot, now I'm just mad. I should have gone with my first instinct about him. I knew he was just a self-centered, arrogant frat boy."

Cassie is staring at the floor. I can only imagine what's going through her head after my story.

"I think he's just scared," she says sympathetically. Is she kidding me right now?

"I can't believe you're making excuses for him. You're supposed to be on my side," I exclaim.

"I am on *your* side. Just promise me that you won't rule things out just yet," she begs.

Um, hell no, I won't make that promise to her. I hope to never see Trevor Ericson again for as long as I live.

After we have our little discussion, we rejoin our parents and Mark in the *game room*. It's actually just a family room but dad insists we should call it the game room. Mom mentions that they're going back to the house for one final walkthrough.

"Do you girls want to see it one more time?" Cassie looks at me and raises her eyebrows. She knows I do.

"Sure," I reply nonchalantly. I don't want to admit out loud that I want to say good-bye forever to my childhood home. Someone might suggest I need professional help. Even though that may not be such a bad idea after thinking about it. I suppose that therapy is probably better than excessive amounts of wine.

We plan to meet at the house in a few days, and I'm absolutely dreading it. I also have to get around to meeting with Lucy to give her my resignation. I'm so glad that she usually takes a vacation right after the recital, so she's been gone while all of this has been going down. She will be returning within the next few days and she will be ready to do the new schedules. I guess the timing couldn't be better.

Cassie pulls me aside right before I decide to head out on my long journey home. "You never told me how things ended with Trevor, when do you think you'll see him again?"

Did she not hear a word I said about my coffee date?

"If I have my wish, I will never see Trevor Ericson ever again. Does that answer your question?" I fold my arms to show that I'm serious.

She raises her eyebrows. "You never know what the future holds, so never say never." Whatever. I may not know everything that the future holds for me, but I do know that it most definitely doesn't include Trevor.

The next week is a complete whirlwind. First and foremost, I had to say a final good-bye to my childhood home. I'm proud to say that I didn't cry—until I drove away—and then it got ugly. As I slid one last time through the house, I felt like I was literally in a slide show of my life. I remember playing with my cousins, enjoying parties and holidays with family, so many good memories. Mom insisted on making us take a picture of every room. I could see that she was also struggling with saying good-bye, and it took all my strength not to say I told you so. I actually think she may be regretting their decision; I knew this would happen at some point. But like the good daughter I am, I kept my mouth shut because I definitely don't need any more lectures from Cassie.

I was feeling totally depressed until Miranda called me with some great news. She set up a time for me to go to New York to meet Selena and tour the studio next week. And the best news is that two of the other instructors will be in need of another roommate very soon. Everything seems to be really coming together for my move. I'm starting to get more excited but still not as much as I thought I would be. I'm hoping that once I visit I will be more excited.

"I wonder what those girls are like?" Georgie asks. She's sitting Indian-style on the floor in the middle of my room looking through a pile of clothes that I'm going to give away. "Doesn't that freak you out? I mean, what if one of them turns out to be a complete psycho or like Ash? That would really suck."

As much as I love Georgie, sometimes I wish she wasn't so honest. The scary part is that she's absolutely right—you never know what people are really like until you live with them. She was lucky enough that one of her friends at the hospital is looking for new place to live, so she at least knows her soon-to-be roommate.

"Yes, it freaks me out, but what other choice do I have?" I exclaim. "And to answer your question, I think I'd rather have a complete psycho as a roommate than someone like Ash. At least you would know that person was psycho. Ash is really deceitful and manipulative and I think that is way more dangerous."

"Damn, that's bad," she says as she is reading the tag on a shirt. "So, you never told me what Ash had to say about the new job. I'm sure the green-eyed monster came out on fire."

I try to pretend like I didn't hear her by *busily* looking through a drawer. I haven't given my notice to Lucy yet but not because I don't want to but because she was on vacation. Granted, I know she got back a few days ago because she sent out a group email asking us to put together our new schedule plans. So maybe I'm avoiding the inevitable.

"Did Ash say anything?" Georgie asks again. Crap, she never just drops things.

"I actually haven't resigned yet," I say slowly. "But in my defense, Lucy just got back from vacation; I know I need to go see her in the next few days."

Her eyes get big. "Oh wow—that's going to be fun," she says sarcastically. I nod my head.

"Yeah, I'm dreading it. You want to come with me?" I smile sweetly. Another option would be to get on my hands and knees and beg her to come.

"Um, yeah, I'm really busy." She gets up and practically sprints out of my room. A few minutes later, she leaves to go meet the dreamy Dr. Scott and I continue to look through my clothes. I hear my phone ringing and find it still in my bag.

I cringe when I see that Beatrice is calling me. I haven't

seen or spoken to her since Trevor brought her to the recital. I have to try my best not to tell her what an ass her precious grandson really is. No matter what, I really like Beatrice so I won't let my disdain for him affect my friendship with her.

"Where have you been hiding, young lady?" she says as soon as I answer the phone.

"Hi, Beatrice. How are you?" I say cheerfully. I'm silently praying she doesn't talk about Trevor.

"Would you believe that I spent an hour on the phone today with The Pottery Barn?"

Who calls it *The* Pottery Barn?

"Katherine ordered me some items and I was trying to make some exchanges. I don't know where they find these people that answer the phone." Beatrice continues to ramble and I let her. Any topic is better than her grandson. Of course, that doesn't last.

"Have you heard the great news?" she asks excitedly. "It's the best news of the year. Trevor finally got rid of that bitch Giselle! I have to say that now I will be able to die in peace. I would never have been able to rest knowing that she had her trampy gold-digging hooks in him. Isn't that the best news?"

Even though I have to agree that it's great news, I'm still trying to figure out a way to get off the phone and fast. Maybe I should tell her that we have a bad connection and I can't hear her. Not like that would do any good because she would just bring it up again the next time we talk. I guess the only way to change the subject is to tell her about my new job.

"I have some great news of my own," I say excitedly.

She listens as I tell her all about Miranda and my new job and, lo and behold, the subject switches back to Trevor. "Does Trevor know about this?"

Hmmm . . . maybe I should tell her it was her bastard grandson's idea. He may even throw me a good-bye party.

"Yes, he does know and he was very supportive," I reply. "In fact, he told me that he thought it was a great decision for me to go and he's absolutely right." Even though I'm still pretty mad at Trevor, he was right. I guess I should appreciate his honesty?

"As smart as my grandson is, that boy has no common sense. I'm going to call him and tell him that he's a stupid idiot." She's practically yelling into the phone. I should probably calm her down, even though it would be pretty amazing to see her tell Trevor off because he deserves it.

"Beatrice, please don't," I beg. "I'm really excited about this opportunity and I've been hoping for something like this to come along for as long as I can remember."

I manage to calm her down and she makes me promise to come visit her before I leave and say good-bye because, according to her, she's ninety and she could die any minute. I really hate comments like that.

"Don't say things like that," I scold her. Now that I've

gotten to know her, it's almost as if Grandma is here with me. I know she's kidding—at least, I think she is. All of a sudden, I start to feel really uncomfortable. I hurry off the phone, promising to set up a time to say good-bye. When I hang up, I feel emotional and I really hate being emotional. Maybe it's just all these life changes or maybe it's hearing Beatrice talk about all that serious stuff. Either way I can't worry about it—I have a bright new future ahead to look forward to, and soon Trevor Ericson will be nothing but a distant memory.

# Chapter 21

"There's my star," Lucy says as she pulls me into to a tight hug. It almost feels like she's suffocating me.

I finally realized that I had to stop putting this off, so I texted Lucy that I wanted to meet with her. Thankfully, she didn't ask any questions. I'm more nervous than I expected I would be. My palms are sweating and my mouth is dry.

"Can we just talk about the artistry of your solo? I mean, I'm still completely mesmerized by that performance." Lucy continues her praising and compliments, making my resignation even more difficult. Before I have a chance to say a word, she hits me with something I definitely wasn't expecting.

"That performance made me realize that you're the person to take over for me and run Do-Re-Mi Studios." She stops and starts to tear up. "I'm not going anywhere just yet, but I know that you would carry on with my heart and soul for this studio." This just keeps getting worse and I need to hurry and give her the bad news.

"Wow, Lucy, that's really kind of you." I smile warmly at her. "I'm honored that you would think so highly of me." I look at her sitting there watching me so proudly. It almost feels as if my mom is sitting on the other side of the desk and that makes this even harder. I look down at the carpet and this time I'm tearing up.

"Lucy, I have something to tell you." The next few minutes are extremely hard and the crying gets a little ugly (not as ugly as it was after saying good-bye to my parents' house) but still not pretty. Lucy is speechless and her proud smile has turned into a look of confusion and then sadness.

"Oh. I had no idea you were even thinking of leaving. When is this *move* going to take place?" she asks softly.

"I'm hoping to leave in about three weeks."

"Oh," she replies shortly. "I remember you always wanted to go to New York but I guess I thought you had made your home here with us."

"I did, and I do feel like you're my family, but this is something I've always wanted and I finally decided to do it." I tear up again. "Believe me, this decision has completely turned my life upside down."

"I'm sorry but I can't just let you go," she exclaims. "Is this because of what happened with Ash and Mimi? Just tell me what I can do to make it up to you."

Although I was hurt by the way things went down with Ash and Mimi, I know I would have made this decision regardless. Of course, my frustration with that situation helped to push me along. I try to assure Lucy that I didn't make this decision because of what happened, and I tell her that there's nothing that will change my mind, at least not right now.

"Well, I can tell you I don't appreciate Miranda recruiting a member of my team," she says firmly. I can see that her confusion has now turned to frustration. Lucy doesn't like losing anything, especially the person whom she was planning to pass along her studio to.

"I'm sorry, Lucy. I hope that you can understand." I'm completely at a loss for words because things have gotten extremely weird all of a sudden. I knew this wasn't going to be easy, but it's actually worse than I expected it would be.

"I do," she says shortly. "I'm expecting that you will be contacting your students and their families to let them know of your plans."

I was going to . . . well, kind of. In the back of my head I was expecting (and hoping) that Lucy would just contact them and assign them to Ash. Our meeting is abruptly cut short when Lucy receives a call. I practically sprint out of her office just to escape the negative energy. Cassie must really be rubbing off on me. As I make my escape, I run smack into Ash of all people. Admittedly, I feel a twinge of excitement.

"Oh, sorry Ash," I say slyly. She rolls her eyes at me. All at once the moment I've been waiting for has been perfectly laid out in front of me. She starts to walk past me toward her closet-office.

"Wait, Ash," I call. She turns around and folds her arms. "I've been thinking, since the recital was such a success maybe it's time for you and me to move on from the past, maybe call a truce?" She doesn't respond. "Especially since I'm leaving," I add. Ash's eyes get wider and her mouth hangs open.

"What do you mean you're leaving?" she asks snidely. "Are you crazy? Lucy thinks you walk on water, especially after you performed your song. Let's be honest, the rest of us had to compete with you before but now after that none of us stand a chance next to you." Her complaining is ruining my moment.

"Well, you won't have to *compete* with me for much longer. As I said, I'm leaving—moving to New York." I must have piqued her interest.

"So, you've turned into one of those silly girls who thinks they will make it in the Big Apple? I definitely didn't expect that from you."

What does she mean by that? I always thought I've been pretty open about my plans to eventually make it there.

"Haha, not exactly," I reply. "I have a really great opportunity and I'm excited about it. Miranda has really gone above and beyond for me." The mention of Miranda definitely sparks something in Ash.

"Miranda? What did she do for you?" she demands. I knew that would get her going. I want so badly to gloat and brag, but I'm a firm believer in karma and I don't need any more negativity in my life right now.

"She gave me some great contacts," I reply shortly. "Anyway, as I was saying, why don't we call a truce?"

I hold out my hand to her. She stares at it as if it was infected with some horrible disease. She slowly grabs my hand and we shake, I doubt even the slightest bit of sincerity but at least I made the effort. She doesn't say another word and rushes off to her closet-office. That wasn't as fun as I thought it would be, but it did give me a small sense of satisfaction.

On my way home, I stop off at this quaint little café to meet up with Georgie and a few of her nurse friends. Apparently, it's become a regular place for women to meet dreamy doctors. I admit I get a little jealous when I arrive watching Georgie and her new friends. I know that sounds totally high school-ish, but I can't help but feel that way. I'm the one who's moving away, so it's silly to expect her not to have new friends. I'm sure I will make lots of new friends as well. I must be standing there daydreaming for a while because the next thing I know Georgie is waving me over.

"What the hell were you doing over there?" she asks. "I've been calling you for five minutes." She giggles.

"What? Oh, sorry." I follow her to her table with her friends. Hayley from the girls' dinner is there. I can tell she has had more than a few drinks because she runs up to me and throws her arms around me as if we're long-lost best friends. "Maris! I'm so happy to see you. Georgie says you're leaving us to go to New York to get famous." Did she say leaving *us*? I didn't know I was leaving *her*.

"I don't know about the famous part, but I am heading to New York." I order a drink and sit down at the table. Hayley sits down next to me and continues with her questions.

"Can we come stay with you? I've never actually been to the city." She takes a sip of her drink. "I really want one of those crowns that looks like the Statue of Liberty. Will you get me one?" This girl must be really drunk because there is no way in hell that I will be seen buying one of those crowns. I need to blend in when I get there. I want to be a true New Yorker and not look like a silly tourist.

"You can get one when you come visit," I say with an innocent smile. I very subtly move away from Hayley and over to Georgie.

"Well, I did it; I gave my resignation to Lucy."

"Ohhh—how did she take it?" she asks while awkwardly looking around.

"Not well, she kept mentioning how upset she was with Miranda for recruiting one of her team. I'm a little nervous she might call her or do something crazy."

"Really?" she asks, still looking preoccupied.

"Who are you looking for?" I ask, abruptly changing the subject. She finally drags her attention back to me. "Sorry, Hayley told me earlier that Candace was bringing Giselle tonight. I was trying to run inter-ference, you know because of the whole Trevor thing," she says, waving her hand.

Oh goody, Giselle. This is going to be a super fun night.

"Maybe I should just leave. I mean, I don't want things to be awkward for you and your friends," I reply sadly.

"What? No way."

Just then, as if she was reading our minds, Giselle walks in. Her outfit doesn't disappoint, as it is a skin-tight black leather halter-top and painted on black leather pants. Maybe Giselle has a double life as an escort.

All of a sudden, I don't want to face her because she probably thinks that Trevor dumped her for me and obviously that couldn't be further from the truth. There is no time for me to sneak out since they are headed straight for us.

"Hey, ladies," Georgie says cheerfully. She and Candace give each other a hug and even Giselle leans in with an air kiss. I follow her lead with giving Candace a hug and then the most awkward moment of my life as Giselle and I face each other. I feel like we are all in slow motion.

"Maris, so good to see you." Giselle leans in for an air kiss to me also. I mindlessly lean in toward her. And then it comes. "I suppose you've heard that Trevor and I are no longer together," she says nonchalantly. "I'm sure Beatrice opened her big mouth. It's for the best though, I really don't have time to deal with all his issues." A bit of relief washes over me, I really wasn't emotionally ready to handle a you-stole-my-man scene in public.

"Honestly, Trevor is not capable of being in a committed relationship, he's a hopeless flirt who gives every woman he meets the idea that he *likes* them. I've seen him do it so many times." Ouch. Now I really feel like such a fool.

"I didn't know you broke up. I'm sorry." I hesitate. Georgie gives me a judge-y look. Oh please, like she has never lied to escape an uncomfortable situation.

"No need to be sorry. Best thing that could have happened." The server brings her a martini and she quickly takes a sip. "Be careful, Maris, he may try to pursue you next." I had a feeling this was coming at some point in this conversation.

"Well, there's not much of a chance of that happening because I'm moving to New York," I say excitedly. And I do feel excited, finally.

Giselle smirks. "Don't tell Trevor because he may follow you there." I'm completely taken aback by that comment. Giselle must get bored talking to me because before I know it she's off leaving a trail of stares from every man she passes.

"What was that all about?" Georgie asks. "She obviously knows that Trevor likes you, otherwise she wouldn't have gone to so much trouble to badmouth him."

I just nod my head. I still feel like an idiot. I was ready to give Trevor a chance, even over Kyle, and it turns out he's just a big player.

"You don't believe any of that stuff she said, do you?" she asks me. "She's obviously lying."

I shake my head. "It doesn't matter anyway, Trevor Ericson is out of my life," I say firmly. "Let's go get a drink."

I don't mean to drink this much. I guess all the stress has finally caught up to me. I end up telling the bartender all my dirty laundry. I tell him everything about my parents' house, Kyle, Trevor (although I change his name to Trenton) just in case there are any spies listening in, and even about my dream with Grandma. That's when he cuts me off—I guess as soon as you mention a ghostly visit they realize that your consumption of alcohol has reached dangerous levels. Georgie takes my keys and drives me home.

"You're my bessst friend," I slur as I'm in and out of falling asleep. She says something but I can't understand it as I drift off.

# Chapter 22

I feel exhilarated as I walk out of Penn Station. New Yorkers are rushing past me but I stand still and take it all in. The day has finally arrived for me to meet Selena, my new roommates, and visit my new studio. I've been so busy packing and organizing that this trip completely snuck up on me.

When I arrive at Selena and Company, I admit I'm a little disenchanted. The outside of the building looks a bit rundown. I start to panic—what if this is a huge mistake? Thankfully, when I walk inside my faith is restored. The inside is gorgeous with big cozy couches and random chandeliers hanging from the ceiling. I approach the receptionist and introduce myself.

"Maris Forrester, we've been expecting you." She gives me a very warm welcome. "You can have a seat. Would you like a mimosa?" I kindly decline—after my drunken night out with Georgie and friends, I have sworn off alcohol for a long time, maybe even forever.

While I semi-patiently wait, I look around the waiting

area. I'm really impressed despite the fact that the outside of the building looks like a complete dive.

"Maris?" I look up to see a really pretty woman, probably in her midfifties. "We finally meet. Come on back to my office." I follow her down a long hallway. When I walk into her office, I'm speechless. First of all, it's huge; you could probably fit three of Lucy's offices inside here. And the view, there's nothing like a New York City skyline view.

"So, as I told you on the phone, Miranda had sent me the video of your performance. Ah-mazing! We're very fortunate that you've agreed to join our team here." I zone out as Selena gives me the rundown of her studio. I don't want to tell her that I've already done my research so I'm already very familiar with the history.

"Ready to see your office?" I come back to reality even though I don't really care about what my office looks like. After spending so many years in a closet-office, I have learned to live with anything. I follow her down another hall. "Here you go." She holds open the door to a room that looks only a tiny bit smaller than hers, and once again the view is fantastic.

"Um, this is mine?" I ask.

"It sure is."

I think I might cry but before I have a chance we are interrupted.

"Are you Maris?" a really tall girl with a thick New York accent asks. "I'm Emma." For a minute, I'm completely lost until I remember that Emma is going to be one of my new roommates.

"Yes. Hi, Emma." I feel totally stupid that I couldn't remember who she was.

"You're coming to see the place tonight, right?" she says while looking at her phone. "I will be there until eight and Angie should be home most of the night. Text when you're heading over." She walks away.

"Nice to meet you," I call.

"You, too." Okay, so she's not really into small talk. I'm sure we will get to know each other better once we're living together.

I spend the rest of the afternoon with Selena. She goes through the student profiles and asks me to make a list of students I would be interested in mentoring. I really like the way she runs the studio—the students are mentored as she calls it (not taught) by all of the instructors because she feels that they can learn something from each one of us. Ash would absolutely hate it here.

When I'm finally on my way to my new apartment, I start to get really anxious. I'm trying not to worry about Emma and her disinterest in meeting me. She was obviously just busy. When I arrive, I take a deep breath and plaster a goofy smile on my face. I really need to figure out a way to get rid of this goofy smile because these New Yorkers will eat me alive with this smile.

I knock several times on the door and nobody answers it. I double-check my phone to make sure I have the right address. I knock again a little harder this time. I'm about to call Angie or Emma when the door flings open.

"You Maris?" the girl whom I assume is Angie asks. I nod my head. "Sorry, I was in the shower and I don't know what Emma's doing. Come in." I follow her in and look around at the very small apartment. They have it decorated nicely but it's definitely not Monica's apartment from *Friends*.

"I'm Angie," she says cheerfully. She shows me around the apartment, which takes a total of ten seconds and finally takes me to my room. To say it's small is an understatement. My new office is bigger—maybe I should just sleep there. I should be able to fit my bed and dresser in here, at least I hope.

"So, rent is due on the first, you have to let the water run for about five minutes to get the hot water, and we do a have an honorary pet mouse—we named him Mickey."

My heart sinks at the thought of mice and who knows what else. What am I doing here? Angie can read my face. "Don't worry, you will get used to Mickey. Welcome to New York," she announces theatrically.

I chat with Angie for about an hour, mostly about the studio. Angie teaches vocal, piano, guitar, and she also teaches modern dance at the nearby dance school. She has a strong passion for the arts, which I can totally relate to. Emma finally comes out of her room, she quickly says good-bye on her way out. Angie explains that she sings at an upscale lounge/bar in SoHo.

"She's trying to make it *big,* if you know what I mean,"

Angie says knowingly. "We all know how that goes though." She giggles

"Yeah." I agree.

"I give her credit, though, she hasn't given up yet. I gave up on that dream a long time ago."

I smile and look around the apartment. I really hope I made the right decision.

When I return to my hotel, I'm exhausted both mentally and physically. I will need to get used to all the walking. I guess I can count this as my new workout plan. I call Georgie to tell her about my day, and of course it's no surprise that the only thing she can focus on is Mickey the mouse. I should have never told her about that, now she will probably never want to visit.

"Are you sure you still want to go? Or maybe you should keep looking for a place to live?" I wish she wouldn't say things like that, it makes me second-guess my decision and that stresses me out.

"On another note, I have to tell you something," Georgie says. I don't like her tone. "I saw Trevor out last night. He came over to me and was asking about you. I told him you were in New York checking out your new job and apartment."

I don't know why but this really pisses me off. Who does he think he is to be asking about me? He made his feelings very clear.

"Whatever."

"I know you aren't going to like me saying this but I think he really cares." She's absolutely right; I don't like it. I'm really glad I'm not sitting next to her right now or I would slap her. Georgie can't possibly be as stupid and naïve as I am.

"Hmm . . . let me guess. Did Trevor use his charm and winning smile to make you believe that? He's really convincing, trust me." I guess Giselle was right. Gag! I can't believe I actually agreed with something Giselle said.

"No. He didn't seem like he was putting on an act. In fact, I felt like he really meant it. He said he was proud of you for following your dreams." I'm so tired and I really don't want to discuss this anymore, so I make up an excuse to get off the phone. I know Georgie means well and I'm sure that there's a part of Trevor that does care, but my pride is so hurt and I just can't get past that, at least not right now.

Regardless, I can't waste any more energy on this—I have a bright new future in the most amazing city in the world and I'm not going to worry about what Angie says. I look out the window at all the bright lights. She may have given up but I'm not going to. I'm going to make it here.

~*~*~

"Really? A good-bye party?" I'm busily packing some boxes when Georgie rushes in with her big plans for a good-bye party. After visiting my new apartment, I realized that there was no way I would be able to bring all my stuff. Thankfully, Cassie is letting me store some things in her garage.

"Of course," she exclaims. "Did you really think I would let you skip town without a party?" She's right. I should have known better.

"I guess not, but you have to pinky promise that you won't go crazy." She smiles and raises her eyebrows, but she still manages to hold out her pinky.

"You're leaving all this stuff at Cassie's?" she asks. "Is your apartment really that small?" She really has no idea. I just hope I don't get claustrophobia.

"Yes, it is. So don't judge." She quickly shakes her head but I know she already started judging as soon as she heard about the pet mouse.

"I will definitely miss this place and my huge closet." I look around feeling emotional again. "But I don't plan on living in that tiny apartment forever. I have plans and goals, and it's just a temporary situation." I think I'm trying to convince myself as well. Georgie wanders around my room touching everything. That used to drive me crazy, but I think I'm going to miss it. She picks up Grandma's journal and starts flipping through it.

"You know the more I think about it, it really is ironic that yours and Trevor's grandmothers were best friends." I give her a dirty look. "Please don't start in with this again."

"Sorry." She scrunches up her face. She's such a liar because I know she's not sorry. A few minutes later, she leaves to take a call from Dr. Scott. I need to remember to thank him the next time I see him for pulling her away from this conversation.

I make my way back to my park. I'm really going to miss this place—hopefully I will find a new place to sing and relieve my stress.

"I'm proud of you."

I turn around and I feel like my heart could burst. "Grandma, you're back!"

She laughs. "I never left."

"I'm doing it. I'm going to New York," I tell her. She smiles and nods her head slowly. "I know, my darling. Just keep following your heart."

"I don't know what you mean by that. I'm not in a relationship anymore." I still don't know if she is referring to a relationship when she talks about that.

"You will figure it out. I have to go now but remember I'm always with you." She starts to walk away but I try to stop her. Somehow deep down I know this is the last time I will be seeing her.

"I love you, my darling."

I sit up and sure enough I'm back in my bed. When I turn on the light, I find Grandma's journal open on the nightstand. I read the last entry again. I smile to myself—for the first time in a long time I'm confident that I'm making the right choice.

# Chapter 23

"I told you not to go crazy," I yell at Georgie. We're back on the fabulous rooftop thanks to Liv and of course Georgie who went overboard planning my good-bye party.

"You know me better than that."

She's absolutely right, I do. Even though I act like I wish she didn't go to all the trouble, I'm so happy to see everyone—my parents, Cassie, Mark, Sophie, Liv, Tom, Dr. Scott, and even a few of my students, including Mimi. I go around the room visiting and thanking everyone for coming.

"This is a hell of a party, much better than that party I had to go to for my birthday." I turn around to see Beatrice. I give her a huge hug.

"Thank you for coming." I do a scan of the room and thankfully Trevor is nowhere to be seen. She must also be able to read minds just like Cassie.

"He dropped me off." She smirks. I give her a questioning look. "Trevor, he dropped me off," she clarifies. "He said to wish you luck."

"Tell him I said thanks," I say shortly. I don't even bother to lie and say I wasn't looking for him. Luckily, my mom comes over to see Beatrice, which saves us from the awkwardness. I feel kind of guilty; maybe I'm being harder on Trevor than I should be. I always hated the fact the Kyle wasn't supportive of my dreams but Trevor comes along and is supportive and I get mad at him. Of course, I was more upset that he rejected me and he made me feel like he didn't care and like I was just another woman for him to play games with.

"Right, honey?" Mom says, looking at me. I was so caught up in my thoughts that I didn't hear her. "What?"

"Beatrice's grandson dropped her off, I called him and told him to come back to the party right away. He should be here, too, he's family." I glare at Beatrice who's innocently looking around the room. That was a sneaky move on her part.

"Whatever," I say through gritted teeth. Surely Trevor would know better than to crash my party despite the annoying prodding that my mother is famous for. I stomp off in a very spoiled brattish kind of way. I remind myself that I was just feeling guilty for being hard on him, so it's time to be a big girl and get over myself already. I guess I will have to abandon my no more drinking rule, at least for this party.

I'm standing at the bar when Georgie rushes over to

me. "Um, Maris, I swear I didn't invite him, you have to believe me." I take a long sip of my (second) drink. "I know, you can thank Beatrice and my mother for that one." She lets out a sigh of relief.

"It's fine, Georgie. I really don't care that he's here; it's about time I get over it anyway." Just because Trevor is here doesn't mean that I have to hang out with him or even talk to him.

I'm actually having a great time at this party. The DJ is fantastic and we're all dancing the night away, no doubt my three (I think?) drinks have helped to calm my nerves.

"Hi." I turn around to see Trevor standing there looking like a Greek god. Was he always this attractive or am I really drunk? "I was hoping we could talk."

He wants to talk? I hope it's not like the last time he wanted to talk.

"Okay." I walk over to a quiet corner. He follows me silently. I turn around and face him, and then I have complete throw up of the mouth.

"Before you say anything, I need to apologize. I may have overreacted slightly that day at Starbucks. I was just so confused about everything and I took it out on you." I guess he didn't expect my apology because he opens his mouth and nothing comes out. Seriously though, was he always this hot? Why am I thinking this? It's my own fault for drinking again.

"Thanks." He shifts his weight from one foot to another. "Now it's my turn, I'm sorry for what I said.

I was giving you mixed signals but only because I was scared of my feelings for you. I didn't want to mess things up, especially after the disaster I had with Giselle. Maris, I really, really like you." We both stand there awkwardly and I'm ignoring the fact that I really have to go to the bathroom.

"I like you, too." I smile.

"So," he says. "What do you think?"

I hate to ruin the moment but I'm about to pee my pants. "I have to go to the bathroom," I say. "Be right back."

Oh my gosh, oh my gosh, oh my gosh. I hurry to the bathroom with Cassie right at my heels. "What's going on? Mom and Beatrice are over in the corner whispering as if they're plotting to take over the world."

I rush into the stall as I tell her about my conversation with Trevor.

"Interesting," she says. "What do you want to do?"

I come out of the stall. "I want to go to New York and do what I love." She smiles and I can tell she's happy with that answer.

"And what about Trevor?" she asks.

I shrug my shoulders. "We'll see, I have to go back and finish our conversation."

I hurry back to Trevor who's still standing in the same

spot I left him in. "Sorry, nature called."

We stand next to each other looking out into open sky. "You know, I think this is where we first met," he says finally. I look around and he's right. "Wow, I think you're right."

We stand there in more silence. "So, can I come to visit you in New York?" he asks.

I turn to face him. "I would really like that." We move closer to each other and he cradles my face in his hands and kisses me. It's just as amazing as I remember it being.

I don't know where things will go with us, but I definitely won't mind him coming to New York and kissing me. Maybe I will finally have that magical moment on top of the Empire State Building— Georgie will be so thrilled.

Before Trevor and Beatrice leave, she pulls me aside. "I'm sorry I had to resort to such desperate measures but you both were being ridiculous. You shouldn't ignore something that's beating you over the head."

I shake my head. "Don't get any crazy ideas, remember I'm moving and I'm not really interested in a long-distance relationship. I need to focus on my career."

She gives me a serious look. "You really are just like your grandmother."

"Thank you. I take that as a compliment." We both laugh and I start to feel emotional again, and I know the next few days aren't going to get any easier. I look around the room at all the people I love. No matter where I live, I know that they will all be here for me anytime I need them and knowing that gives me comfort that everything will be okay.

# Chapter 24

"Get out, get out, get out," I scream. I've been in New York for one week and Mickey the mouse has come out to welcome me quite a few times. Emma and Angie keep reminding me that I will get used to it, but I admit I haven't gotten much sleep. I swear he and his gross little friends are all running around my room as soon as the lights go out.

My last few days at home were really hard, especially saying good-bye to Georgie and my family. My dad and I drove the truck with the few items that barely fit into my new room. I can tell my dad wasn't impressed with my new living space, but I assured him it would only be temporary until I have a chance to look around for something bigger (and nicer).

I love my new studio and I really wish I could just move into my office. It's spacious and rodent-free. Unfortunately, my first week hasn't gone as smoothly as I had hoped. Apparently, Lucy contacted Miranda and Selena and threatened to sue them for recruiting me. She's claiming I signed some sort of contract, which I never did. Miranda says she has a meeting with her lawyer and everything will be fine. I started to panic when Selena said that she had no interest in getting involved in some big legal issue. I knew that Lucy was upset about me leaving but I had no idea she would go down this route.

After my two lessons this morning, I decide to take a walk down the street to a little deli that Angie recommended. I sit down with my lunch and pull out my phone. Georgie has been texting me day and night asking how things are going. I've been keeping her updated leaving out my welcome party from the mice. I don't want to admit to her that I'm really homesick and lonely. I know it's only been a week and it will get easier as time goes on. My roommates are nice but that's exactly what they are, roommates. They each have their own separate lives and friends.

"Maris?" I look up to see who knows my name. I'm completely shocked to see Kyle, standing next to me in this tiny New York deli. Am I dreaming again?

"Kyle? What are you doing here?" I realize that I'm yelling at the top of my lungs and several people look over. A few roll their eyes at me in the typical New Yorker kind of way.

"I'm in the city for work again. May I sit down?"

I'm so happy to see Kyle. We haven't spoken since things ended for us and there have been many times that I wanted to call him just to see how he was doing. I was sitting here feeling really lonely, so it's nice to see a familiar face.

"Of course." I motion for him to sit down. He pulls out the chair across from me. "How are you? How's the job?" I ask eagerly.

We chat about his job, family, and my new job. It feels like old times before all the confusion and *what are we doing with our lives* stuff got in the way.

"I'm really proud of you, you made this happen, and I admire that more than you know." He smiles and looks down at his hands the way he always does when he gets nervous.

"Thanks. I appreciate . . ." He interrupts me. "I have to tell you the truth." He announces looking up from his hands. "I didn't just randomly show up in this deli. I found out where you worked from Georgie and I went to the studio and they told me that you came here for lunch." He looks so stressed out as if he has admitted his guilt to some horrible crime.

"Wow. Are you stalking me?" I ask sarcastically, trying to lighten the mood.

"Maybe?" he laughs. "But honestly, I miss you and now it looks like I'll be traveling here more for work so I wanted to know if we could try things—I know it's not an ideal situation, but I'm willing to try it. Would you?"

What just happened? Am I hallucinating? Kyle continues talking. "I made so many wrong decisions— asking you to move in with me and then proposing to you. I was trying to force you to stay and that was wrong. I knew all along that you wanted to come here and I was trying to hold you back." He moves his chair around the table next to me. He leans his head in and whispers in my ear. "We're good together in so many ways." He winks as I sit with my mouth still hanging open. "Let's try this again, I know we can do this," he begs.

All of a sudden, the memories come flooding back to me. I remember the way he took care of me after I had my wisdom teeth taken out, I remember the scent of his cologne and of his peppermint breath. (Seriously, Kyle *never* has bad breath.) But at the same time, I remember how frustrated I felt when he didn't support my dreams. Maybe we can do this, but take things slow? Not to mention Trevor is still a part of my life waiting in the wings. I can't ignore my feelings for him either. Oh hell, is it really possible to be in love with two men at the same time? I have to be honest with Kyle.

"I know we're good together," I whisper back. "And I want to say yes, but I have to be honest with you about something. I still care about you but I care about someone else, too." He sits straight up in his chair. "Are you already seeing someone else? I thought you just got here?"

I shift around in my chair. "No, not exactly. I mean, there is someone else that I have a connection with." Ugh, I hate using Trevor's stupid term. "We aren't seeing each other exactly, but we're talking and he's planning a trip to visit me." I trail off. This seems to get more and more complicated and just when I thought I was done with all of it, I'm thrown back in.

Kyle is quiet but I can tell he's trying to process everything. "Fine. I'm still willing to do this. I will just have to win your heart all over again." I don't mean to laugh out loud but I can't help it. He makes it sound as if we're in some old movie and he has to battle another man for my affections. Although, I guess that's not too far from the truth.

"Don't laugh, I'm serious," he says as one corner of his mouth turns up into a half smile. "We will make this work, I know it. I will learn to love this city if I have to. I will eat hotdogs from those disgusting street carts and I will memorize the subway routes. I will even become best friends with that naked cowboy guy. Whatever it takes."

I don't know whether to laugh or cry. The reality is that I'm almost getting everything that I've always wanted except that this time there is someone else thrown in the mix.

"Okay." I agree. Kyle jumps up and punches the air as if he's just won a bunch of money in Vegas. He pulls me up out of my seat and kisses me. I feel like I'm melting again—I still need to Google where that phrase came from. Everyone in the restaurant starts cheering, you'd have thought it was all planned out. If a flash mob starts, then I will completely break down. I grab his hands and we sit back down. "But please understand that right now my main focus has to be my career. That's the reason I'm here. I may not make it, but I have to try."

"Yes, yes, yes. And I will be right by your side to support you . . . or if you need me." He corrects himself.

I smile and throw my arms around him.

Here I go again. If I wasn't losing it before, I am definitely now. I went from some weird sort-of love triangle to having no men in my life and now I'm back at square one. I need to be honest and tell Trevor the same thing I told Kyle. My career is my first focus, but I'm 100% positive that I have feelings for both of them. If Trevor is also willing to be patient with me while I figure all of this out, then we will see what happens. For now, I can take my time and follow my heart in whatever direction it leads me.

## The End

## Dear Reader:

I hope you enjoyed *See You Soon Broadway*. Please take a few minutes to leave a review on Amazon and don't forget to visit my website to sign up for my newsletter.

Stay tuned for my book coming soon!

Authormelissabaldwin.com

Follow me on Facebook, Twitter, and Instagram.

# About the Author

Melissa graduated from the University of Central Florida with a Bachelor's Degree in Communications. She has always had a love for writing. An avid journal keeper, she fulfilled her dream with her debut novel, *An Event to Remember . . . Or Forget.*

Melissa resides in Orlando, Florida, with her husband and young daughter. She is a master at organization and multi-tasking. Her daily jobs include mother, chauffeur, wife, PTA President, fitness trainer, and author.

When she has free time, she enjoys traveling, fitness, decorating, fashion, and taking a Disney Cruise every now and then.